THE

THE TEACHER'S HAND-POOK

Besides being another hilarious yarn in the series, *The Teacher's Hand-Pook* voices a plea from many teachers who are worried by the sometimes unhelpful programmes, methods and theories imposed upon them from above by folks not directly in the firing line of modern education. Much of this concern is summed up by that outspoken representative of the Old Guard, Mr Mould, in his Teacher's Prayer:

'Preserve us this day from child psychiatrists, cranky College lecturers, Headmistresses on horseback, crackpot teachers, promotion charlies, do-gooders, education experts, potty parents, comedy writers, and all other persons who do not understand children. Forgive our own Headmaster because he is comparatively harmless.'

Too often these well-meaning schemes which appear so progressive and attractive on paper— have a habit of operating in a completely reverse direction when applied to our pupils in the classroom.

Mr Mould also begs that the public may be protected from the sensation seeking smarties of the mass-media, that they be permitted to think for themselves about their children's education.

And who better to illustrate such disasters than Pook himself, as he plummets into one hilarious pitfall after another in this fascinating panorama of school life—whereby he discovers that children are really small adults with the saving grace of youth.

Peter Pook titles
In the order in which they were originally published

Banking on Form
Pook in Boots
Pook in Business
Pook Sahib
Bwana Pook
Professor Pook
Banker Pook Confesses
Pook at College
Pook's Tender Years
Pook and Partners
Playboy Pook
Pook's Class War
Pook's Tale of Woo
Pook's Eastern Promise
Beau Pook Proposes
Pook's Tours
The Teacher's Hand-Pook
Gigolo Pook
Pook's Love Nest
Pook's China Doll
Pook's Curiosity Shop
Marine Pook Esquire
Pook's Viking Virgins

THE TEACHER'S HAND-POOK

An Introduction to Children
for Teachers, Parents and Education Experts

PETER POOK

EMISSARY PUBLISHING
P.O. Box 33, Bicester, OX26 4ZZ, UK.

First published in Great Britain 1975
by Robert Hale Ltd., London.

First issued in paperback in 1992 by
Emissary Publishing, P.O. Box 33, Bicester, OX26 4ZZ, UK.

This edition published 2008

www.peterpook.com

British Library Cataloguing-in-Publication Data.
A catalogue record for this book is available from the British Library.

ISBN: 978-1-874490-66-1

Produced by: Manuscript ReSearch (Book Producers),
P.O. Box 33, Bicester, OX26 4ZZ, U.K.
Tel: 01869 323447
Printed and bound by MWL Print Group Ltd., South Wales.

To all the delightful children—and teachers—
who wrote this book for me

"I rename this ship *Spirit of Adventure,* and may God bless all who learn in her," Dr Collins informed the assembled school and Governors, breaking a tiny bottle of Lucozade against a brass bell inscribed Royal Sea Nymph, 1879.

I experienced the odd feeling that the entire Assembly Hall with its thousand pupils and staff was sliding backwards down the slipway into the sea as the Headmaster made his launching speech—a speech which failed to include the reason that Dr Collins deemed a change necessary since the mysterious overnight metamorphosis of the name on the ship's bow from *Royal Sea Nymph* to *Royal Sex Nympho.*

"Seldom in educational history has a Governor been so generous to his school as the Honourable Lesley Pilkington-Goldberg, ladies and gentlemen, in that he has seen fit to present to us on permanent loan that magnificent old man-o'-war, that history-soaked guardian of our shores, that bloodstained reminder of our glorious past, which I now have the honour to rename *Spirit of Adventure.*"

"My idea of the spirit of adventure is a bottle of Scotch," Mr Mould growled beside me, "not a broken-down old frigate."

"Try to imagine what joys lie ahead of us, boys and girls, as we practise our woodwork skills repairing the timbers; practise our metalwork skills repairing the anchors; practise our craft skills repairing the sails; practise our art skills gilding the figurehead; practise our mathematics calculating the dimensions; practise our English as we write the story; practise our History as we discover the wars she fought in; practise our Geography as we trace her voyages over the seven seas of the world. . . ."

"Practise our laundry skills washing our clothes when we leave the filthy old wreck," Mr Mould observed to me. "Wake me up when he's been through the whole gamut of the curriculum and tell me how he contrived to fit in Religious Knowledge and

Human Biology, Peter."

Honners, the source of our new nautical bias in education, sat on the dais with the Headmaster trying to look philanthropic and not bored simultaneously. His unique gift to the school of an 1879 naval frigate came under the heading of 'Vintage model in need of repair, suit enthusiast,' as they say in the car trade when outing a banger from stock. Only Honners knew that he could not sell the frigate because of a codicil to that effect in the family trust; could not give her away because of her poor condition; could not break her up due to a preservation order. Moreover, Cudford Council had served Honners with a summons whereby he was required to make such repairs as necessary to comply with the needs of public safety, whereby people might walk along the bank of the river Cud without being crushed under a falling yard-arm, or row past the vessel without being sunk by an insecure davit. Even as he sat there, it occurred to Honners that we might soon be practising our first-aid skills merely by boarding the vessel, but he salved his conscience by including such risk under the ship's new name, *Spirit of Adventure*.

Dr Collins was excited on two counts. First, like most Headmasters he revelled in new toys—although, like most Headmasters, he soon tired of them once they were unpacked and he had discovered how they worked and how easily they broke down. Through him we had changed from a modest hand-operated duplicator to an electrically powered giant capable of producing a small newspaper if necessary. Then there arrived such modern teaching aids as the television and its video-tape-recorder, enabling us to view programmes on how to build a fifteen-mile-long dam to prevent the North Sea engulfing our school; how to divert lava flow in case the school was resited on the slopes of Mount Etna; what to do if you took out a school party and they fell down a crater on the moon; how to augment school dinners by turning the playground into a paddy-field and

10

planting rice. Programmes which, to be frank, bored the children intensely until I accidentally ran the tape backwards to re-wind, and at last they were enthralled to see lava rushing up the slopes of Mount Etna, then leaping into the crater at the summit, followed by alarmed peasants running into their houses and jumping into bed.

"As your school Governor—or as I prefer to regard myself, your beloved Gaffer—I was determined that you and no-one else should benefit by the addition of this proud relic of our Silent Service to your existing educational facilities," Honners impressed upon us in his speech of bequest. "I realize full well how your Headmaster strives to keep Cudford School in the forefront of modern education, but even he must admit that no school in the area can compete with a real man-o'-war riding serenely at anchor within gunshot of this hall."

We all turned our heads to the right to witness such a spectacle, but only the tip of the mainmast was visible over the roof of our new gymnastics and sports hall. This was the second point which excited Dr Collins, who, like many Headmasters, kept his ear to the ground for new educational breakthroughs, good, bad or indifferent, ever ready to jump on the fashionable bandwagon of the hour, ever anxious to appear progressive, ever keen to outstrip other schools in the region. Unfortunately, experience taught us that much of the avant garde methods were devised by well-meaning eggheads far removed from the realities of the classroom so that often what once we were told was white was later classified as black, and methods discredited as bad were sometimes encouraged later as good. We learned, too, that often logical theory which appears so sound in books tend to operate the other way round in practice and produce the opposite effect to what was intended.

A good illustration of this point occurred when Dr Collins took an extra long jump to land on the non-streaming bandwagon. All pupils were to be grouped in classes irrespective of ability, performance or any classification other than age, on the grounds of equal opportunity for all except the staff, because Dr Collins himself did not take any classes.

The result was the unhappiest year I experienced in teaching, and the children loathed it. At one end of a class of 36 pupils were three remedial children who could barely read or write, while at the other extreme were four potential G.C.E. candidates. Class teaching was obviously impossible, so, on Dr Collins' advice, I divided the class into four groups, prepared four separate lessons each day and tried to motivate all four groups on a kind of rota system. The results were disastrous. The top group were aggrieved that their examination chances had been impaired by neglect and told me it had been a largely wasted year. The two middle groups did not know where they were at all.

But the bottom group—whom the threorists had insisted would benefit most—were the hardest hit, ironically enough. They were so discouraged by the comparative brightness of the others that they lost heart and gave up after one term. As for me, I was a nervous wreck and I informed Dr Collins that if he persisted with non-streaming I should be compelled to leave the school. I am all in favour of assisting less able children but I am suspicious of any system which tends to handicap the brighter ones, and I say most sincerely to all educationalists please first prove your theories in the often difficult environment of the classroom, not for a lesson or two but over the year—then come and show front-line teachers like myself how to do it at Cudford Secondary Modern School.

Educational gimmickry affected Mr Mould not at all. "I refuse to believe that if you put a bad apple in a barrel of good apples the latter will turn the bad apple good," he stated. "Unfortunately, Peter, I am an old die-hard of yesteryear who still persists in the outmoded idea that discipline, work and mutual respect between teacher and pupil is the cornerstone of sound education. It is a sobering thought that while these basic principles are approved of by our red friends abroad, our red friends at home decry them most vociferously in relation to our own pupils. We observe with amazement that the rigid, formal and highly disciplined educational systems employed in the countries of our red friends are, they tell us, extremely bad for us in this country and must be scrapped in favour of free discipline, do-as-you please, pupil-controlled curriculums."

"Why should they want that, Mr Mould?"

"I don't know, Peter," Mr Mould replied, lighting his pie, "because I am a simple old schoolmaster not blessed with a suspicious mind. Only last week in Fifth Year discussion, a prefect kindly informed me that in a free society he should have the freedom to choose what subjects he took and who taught him. I agreed, pointing out that as freedom is indivisible I should be able to choose what subjects I taught and whom I taught. I hinted that he might not be on my list of pupils. This view of freedom seemed to catch him off-balance, because often those who are most vociferous about their rights overlook the fact that other people have rights too. 'Go back and ask your clever friends the answer to that one,' I suggested."

"So you do not approve of pupil participation in the running of a school, Mr Mould?"

Mr Mould laughed and drew heavily on his pipe. "I do, I do, Peter. I have been trying to put this new revolutionary idea into practice for the last twenty years. Trouble is I can't get any pupils to participate. At their age they're just not interested, believing, understandably, that it is our job to run the school and their job to do their lessons and play football like normal teenagers. A school committee of two is not good, Peter—especially when the only other attending member is Fred Rubble of the Fourth. Rubble's main concern is the Redistribution of Wealth, by which he means that I should hand over my life savings to his father—a gentleman who does not work because

13

he would actually lose money if he came off National Assistance. I have explained to Rubble that, human nature being what it is, any scheme for the Redistribution of Wealth around the Cudford area would have to operate every three months, because the rich are too mean to spend it and the poor are too shiftless to save it—which explains the modern paradox of the poor often earning more money than the rich."

"So our School Council is defunct, Mr Mould?"

I'm afraid so, Peter. Even Fred Rubble—who is yet another victim of the strains and stresses of modern life, in that he is unable to face the ordeal of washing or getting up in time for school—failed to attend after three meetings, poor lad. However, I canvassed our pupils for suggestions to improve the school, which produced two recommendations. The first one I ignored, not yet being of retirement age, and am now working on the second to provide a swimming-pool for which at present, unfortunately, we have neither room nor money."

Up on the stage of the Great Hall Honners was warming to his theme. "You will be interested to learn, boys and girls, that my illustrious forbear, Admiral Sir Victor Pilkington-Goldberg, V.C., C.B. and sundry foreign decorations, fought the then *Royal Sea Nymph* during the Egyptian War of 1882."

"I didn't realize women were allowed on board," Mr Mould observed to me, "especially the King's mistress."

"During the action of bombarding Alexandria Sir Victor suffered the misfortune of losing his left leg."

"Petty theft is still rife in the navy today," Mr Mould told me. "One wonders how they smuggled it ashore and through the Dockyard gates."

"Is there still a market for left legs, Mr Mould?"

"Only if the Order of the Garter happens to be on it. Otherwise they want both legs for the pair of shoes."

"When you board this historic frigate, boys and girls, the first thing to strike you will be the damage she suffered during that terrible action."

"It will strike you particularly on the head," Mr Mould reflected. "Those Egyptians must have been firing dry rot and death-watch beetles at her."

"But time has not diminished her noble dignity, nor has the cruel scar of battle detracted from her martial beauty. All I ask in return, boys and girls, as you visit her in the pursuit of knowledge and the exploration of skills is that you and your worthy teachers make every endeavour to restore her to those former glories she so richly deserves. Ladies and gentlemen, pupils of Cudford School, I give you—on permanent loan—the good ship *Spirit of Adventure,* and may God bless all who work in her."

"And he doesn't want her back either," Mr Mould commented as the Headmaster called for three rousing and well-rehearsed huzzas from the assembled matelots of Cudford School.

The next day Dr Collins called us into conference—the Board of Admiralty as he dubbed it—to brief us on how the ship was to be integrated into all branches of the syllabus, as though we had suddenly become part of the work force at Upper Clyde Shipbuilders. Admiral Collins himself, I noticed, would not be directly involved in the action but would be ever hovering on the horizon to advise us, encourage us, observe our progress and report our academic breakthroughs to the Ministry of Education, Cudford Education Committee, the teaching unions, Press and Television, the Headmasters' Association and envious schools abroad, under the general heading of The Collins' Approach to New Learning.

"I give it one term," Mr Mould informed me, having asked the Headmaster how his subject of Religious Knowledge would fit into the new scheme and being told to remember Jonah and the Whale and St Paul's shipwreck on the coast of Malta, plus a quote about those whose business is in great waters and Noah building the Ark. "If old Noah had built the Ark like this tub the human race would have been wiped off the face of the earth even before it rained, Peter, and St Paul would have been shipwrecked at the port of embarkation. I shall take as my text, "'The Lord will stretch forth his hand and pull me from the deep'."

"'And deliver me from mine enemy.' How did Dr Collins get his title anyway?"

"Rumour has it that he adopted it many years ago, similar to Dr Lloyd's Wind & Bilious Pills. Others say he trained to be a vet. For my money I reckon it was an honorary degree bestowed on him by an African university and he dropped the witch, thus shortening it to Doctor. Like most Headmasters, Dr Collins possesses one outstanding gift—the ability to excel at interviews for Headships, similar to the Olympic athlete who lifts the heaviest weight, but who, stripped of his barbell, is nothing."

"But he carries a lot of responsibility on his shoulders, Mr Mould."

"Indeed he does, Peter, to the tune of £4,000 a year plus, which enables him to take a firm stand on the fence with both feet firmly planted in the air. So much responsibility, in fact, that he has no time to teach in the classroom, thereby being out of touch with the nub of educational problems, such as children."

"It seems to me, Mr Mould, that our best teachers rise to the top where they no longer teach."

"It is the paradox of our system, Peter. But I must explain in all fairness that the ambition of most staff is to rise high enough in their profession to float out of the classroom for ever, similar to soldiers who strive to leave the front line for a safe job back at base with their Generals. This has always been my goal, but unfortunately, being a simple soul without guile, I have attained only to be Head of Department. That is to say I command an empire of one other member of staff—where I shall remain unless the retirement age is raised to ninety-five."

"Then how did Mr Pearson manage it so young?"

"Ah, Mr Pearson—or, to give him his popular title, Caesar—perceived early in his career that the road to blissful peace in education was to establish a separate state under Dr Collins called Careers Adviser. In this role he is free to advise on and promote his own career, then, if time permits, the careers of our pupils."

"Why is he called Caesar, Mr Mould?"

Mr Mould smiled enigmatically. "Because he is an example to all of us who have failed in our profession, whereby he has built up his own private empire from nothing, until today he is the vital king-pin in the complex organization linking school, employer, parent, pupil and the Youth Employment Officer. So successful a Department that I myself have been tempted to seek employment under the brilliant Mr Pearson as a last desperate throw to escape the rigours of the classroom."

Our conversation was interrupted by the arrival of Dr Collins, who was escorting Honners round the staff in order to show the flag. Mr Mould gave Honners a naval salute and puffed at his pipe.

Dr Collins was in jovial mood. "Ah, Mr Mould, I should like to see old Mitchell's face up at Liddale School when he hears of our new nautical approach to education, eh?"

"No doubt it will register an expression of triumph that the hazard of drowning in the classroom has been added to our other exigencies," Mr Mould commented.

"For months I have been seeking a counter to his Televised Pastoral Care experiment, whereby staff have visited pupils' homes to film-interview parents *in situ*, preparatory to screening the results on the school's closed-circuit television. But in all modesty, I believe our new marine-orientated curriculum will quickly edge him out of the limelight."

"If I may say so, Dr Collins," Honners observed, "Your far-sighted flair for progress may well be such a landmark in education as to revolutionize learning, not only in this country but also throughout the world."

"The only school with a lifeboat rescue service and no staff," Mr Mould suggested.

Dr Collins patted Mr Mould on the shoulder. "I know you are suspicious of new methods, Mr Mould, but we must move with the times."

"I merely point out that change does not necessarily equate with improvement," Mr Mould scowled, "and as for moving with these present times I prefer to disembark and remain with former times, where we knew where we were—which Peter has referred to as the bad old days when people were so much happier than they are now. Those wicked times which lacked the excitement of football hooliganism; when old ladies were not coshed in their beds for kicks, and veterans like myself could walk abroad at night without being mugged by our new knights of the road; when the intelligentsia of our Universities did not see fit to display their talents in drunken anarchy; when our intellectual revolutionaries preferred not to parasite on the state they sought to overthrow, then, like ungrateful pimps, turn against the mistress who supported them; when the trade unions did not cry Democracy! to excuse the use of force against a democratic government; when extremists failed to see how blowing up a crowded supermarket would further their cause; when . . ."

Dr Collins held up his hands. "Gentlemen, you will notice how Mr Mould is not entirely satisfied with present-day affairs."

"Satisfied! Sir, when I observe those people who would save me from imaginary tyranny I flee terror-struck into the arms of the Law. When I observe those people who would liberate me by violence I drop on my knees to beg them not to kill me in the name of Liberty. When I observe those people who would give me peace I pray God I may be spared their good offices, that I may die in my bed."

"My dear Mould, all we are considering at the moment is our

exciting new outward-looking approach to the syllabus, based on our glorious naval heritage."

Mr Mould puffed deeply at his pipe. "Old-fashioned diehard that I am, sir, I do not take kindly to becoming a party in your play-way to illiteracy. I subscribe to the traditional methods of education based on work in the classroom. I am well aware that our red friends exhort us to abandon formal teaching and our anti-social examinations, yet I view with puzzlement how such bourgeoise techniques dominate the educational systems in the countries of their red masters to a degree of regimentation and discipline far in excess of our own. Yes, sir, I am bewildered that what is good for them is bad for us—to the extent that were I a suspicious person I should question their motives. One might well ask them to reform their own systems before bothering with ours. I am reminded of the minister who said he favoured the abolition of the death sentence, but he would like the murderers to make the first move to that end."

I always enjoyed listening to Mr Mould, if only to hear those rolling periods boom from his chest to fill the staff room with his views on every subject; such as Maths—"This morning I discovered young Tom Bilberry smoking in the toilet, his body racked with sloth after the intellectual rigours of classroom bingo."

Despite his strict discipline and rough tongue Mr Mould was liked and respected by the pupils, some of whom requested to join his class in order to enhance their examination and career prospects. His severest critics had to admit he was a master of his trade in every dimension—"What small ability I may possess is based upon labour, experience and common sense; therefore of dubious value in modern education." When asked by a college lecturer why he was so strict with the pupils he replied, "I merely follow the advice of your own Lenin when he said, 'Liberty is so precious that it must be rationed'."

Mr Mould's favourite quotation came from the Bible, 'Ye

shall know them by their works'. This, he claimed, was the criterion of all action, the grand exposé of ulterior motives. Talk is cheap, he often told me; what really counts is what people do. Notice how those who are most vociferous in the cause of free speech are so often the very ones who will hear no voice but their own—silencing opposition by force if necessary. "When I hear people shouting for liberty I suspect they are demanding licence—and I fear for my safety."

Mr Mould never tired of reminding us that 1962 was the turning-point in our history, the year of the Cuban crisis when America and Russia confronted each other with nuclear missiles, "Kennedy and Khrushchev, each with his gun at the other's heart, realized it was the Great Stalemate of history. So our red friends decided to conquer us by subversion. We in this country refuse to believe it because such a policy is laid down in their writings and borne out by their actions, therefore to be dismissed by us as foreign propaganda as we learned to do in the 1930's, when rumour-mongers like Winston Churchill pretended that Hitler was arming for our destruction."

"Your own subject of Religious Knowledge will profit considerably," Dr Collins beamed enthusiastically.

"Only to the extent of giving fresh meaning to the Burial Service at Sea," Mr Mould replied coldly.

"But think of the missionary journeys of the Apostles to spread the Gospels "

"Most of which they sensibly accomplished on foot, sir. If they had undertaken to spread the Word via our present vessel I fear Britain would have been more pagan than she is today."

"Then consider the Fishermen of Galilee, Mr Mould."

"I have considered them for half a century, sir, and envy the immediacy with which divine aid came to their rescue when the storm arose. Unfortunately, my own humble faith may be insufficient to procure similar assistance on the River Cud, even during calm weather. For this venture I shall place my trust nearer home in the policy of Cudford Life Assurance Company."

Dr Collins turned to me for support. "I am certain that you are happy to see the new horizons we have opened up in the quest for knowledge and motivation, Peter."

"Delighted, sir," I replied impassively. I agreed with everything the Headmaster said so I could gain promotion and leave the classroom, but at the same time I did not have to win an Oscar for emotion in the process.

"In what particular direction are you delighted, Peter?"

Dr Collins did not seem satisfied with the narrow confines of my rapture.

"Delighted to see the new horizons you have opened up in the quest for knowledge and motivation, sir." I always quoted his words back to him, on the principle that this was one thing he could not quarrel with, except the substitution of *you* for *we* to give him the credit in the short term and the blame in the long term. As the frigate decision was irrevocable I registered my academic bliss smile to let him see I was not merely delighted and fed up, but ready for promotion on the next tide. I had cultivated a special smile for the Headmaster, which I dubbed 'I'm with you, sir, no matter what the others think,' and he had a special smile for me which read, 'I knew I could count on you, Judas.'

"Ah, Peter, I expect your theme in English next term will be *Sea Fever,* eh?" Dr Collins prompted me archly.

"Or *The Loss of the Royal George,* " Mr. Mould suggested.

"I must go down to the seas again; the lonely sea and the sky. And all I ask is a town school, that's formal, inland and dry," I quoted, in case Dr Collins was getting overconfident.

"Ha, ha! Mr Mould has always assured me that I command a well-oiled team of rebels. Well, that's what education is all about—a microcosm of many opinions. Tell me, Peter, what is your professional ambition?"

"To teach in a C.F. school, sir."

"Is that a Church School?"

"No, sir, a Child-Free School. Ha, ha, ha, ha!" Mr Mould had advised me always to block the Head's staff data probes thus, on the principle that the less he knew about one the better. On the other hand it was the staff's duty to unearth every morsel of information possible about the Head—particularly about his earlier career—so we could analyse the secret of success for our own use, and also hamstring his present hold over our careers.

In this way Mr Mould had built up a detailed reconstruction of the Head's life as from birth, from which he was able to attack his decisions most effectively and even prognosticate his future plans. Mr Mould made no secret of the fact that he played the Duke of Wellington to the Head's Napoleon, 'finding out what you don't know from what you do know'. One of our chief intelligence agents was Mrs Mould, who supported Mrs Collins so enthusiastically on her committee work as to give the impression she was the Head's sister-in-law. But above all Mrs Mould was able to breach Dr Collins' domestic defences, so that, even as he spoke to us now, we knew the size of his pants and how whisky made him snore in bed. Likewise we knew that when he had attacked Germany so courageously in the Second World War that Hitler was forced to capture and imprison him for five years in order to secure the Western Front, Dr Collins was a major in the Pay Corps. Mr Mould said the more you knew about someone the better you loved him, and that we had more soot on Collins than the FBI had on Al Capone.

For example, through our espionage network we learned that Dr Collins was not allowed out at night unless accompanied by Mrs Collins' guard-dog Fang. Nothing sinister in that unless you knew that the landlord of the Bold Forester kept an alsatian called Pickles who permitted no other dog to enter the pub, especially Fang. Fang was a miniature poodle whom the alsatian regarded merely as a barking lamb-chop with legs, and when Dr Collins hurried past the Bold Forester on the other side of the road the alsatian's canine mind obviously could not comprehend why a grown man should walk the streets with a meal hanging from a lead just to torture hungry alsations.

We all remembered that Christmas Eve some time ago when Dr Collins tried to enter the Bold Forester without Pickles knowing by creeping in the Bottle & Jug door, holding Fang on his shoulder like a parrot, disguised in his red winter coat and diamanté collar with matching hair ribbon. Eyes wide and jaws open, Pickles watched from the stairs, unable to believe his good fortune that Father Christmas was delivering his dinner so early—not a big meal but at least a change from tinned meat, and, above all, bark fresh. Being the festive season, Pickles hoped they would let him chase his dinner into his bowl for once, then unwrap it at his leisure, like they did with their own presents.

Pickles waiting politely while Father Christmas took a glass of refreshment, then pantingly during the second, but when the glass went under the Scotch optic for the third time it was more than fur could bear. As was his custom, Pickles entered the Bottle & Jug with an easy bound over the counter, soaring up to six feet in order to survey his dinner at eye-level. Pickles did not regard Fang as an intruder like the airedales and boxers he hauled down from cupboard tops and threw shrieking into the street, but as a yappy little present for his enjoyment who would be fun to chase before supper. Though not as much fun as whippets, who could run so fast that Pickles had to change into overdrive until they had tired sufficiently to be caught.

By any standards Pickles was large, but I was always taken by surprise when he stretched up to his full height, towering over Dr Collins with his dentist's nightmare of a smile which revealed a kind of ivory arsenal up front, as though our Headmaster was supporting an upright shark. Fang's terrible scream of terror brought many hands to the rescue, though Fang himself had to be taken to the vet suffering from a nervous breakdown and hallucinations that he was a highly-strung meat bone with paws. Mrs Collins, who never forgave her husband's deception, declared that Fang's fur had turned white on top of his tiny head and predicted he would go bald within the year.

This trifling incident taught us that Mrs Collins wielded such power over the Headmaster that privately we referred to her as the School Governor, and when Dr Collins tried to tyrannize us we nodded sympathetically because we knew it was mere psychological compensation for his domestic repression. Mr Mould explained to us that behind every successful man stands the female counterpart of Bomber Command on red alert, and that we were to regard Dr Collins as having been flattened as a consequence.

Naturally, we rallied round our Headmaster to protect him from female domination, assuring him that under no circumstances would we exploit such a factor except as blackmail to secure our own ends. Mr Mould possessed much experience in this field because behind him stood the lady he referred to as the Colossus of Rhodes, who, he declared, interpreted the marriage clause 'Till death us do part' as the Church's licence for her to murder him after closing time at the Bold Forester.

However, two members of staff were favourably disposed towards *Spirit of Adventure;* Mr Tadd, the woodwork master, and his friend Mr Figgin, the metalwork master. They liked everything that floated, and what did not float soon did under their skilled hands. In fact, it can be stated as a general proposition that everything which passed through their departments ended up afloat, usually on their two yachts lying at anchor on the River Cud.

Supreme masters of their crafts, Bert Tadd and Sid Figgin put on such a display at Open Days as to compel Mr Mould to designate it as National Boat Week. The boys made beautiful cleats, pulleys, oars, dinghies, balers, boat-hooks and even small anchors for the public's admiration—all of which reappeared later on the two yachts in question, moored in the miniature marina Mr Mould referred to as Upper Clyde Ship-builders. Our examination candidates were the envy of the area as they passed with honours in woodwork and metalwork, with their boats in the former and their yacht trailers in the latter—many of them taking up careers in the Navy, Mercantile Marine and Hovercraft design offices as a matter of course.

Mr Tadd and Mr Figgin eyed *Spirit of Adventure* with almost unnatural zest, like bees getting a bearing on the Chelsea Flower Show.

So Dr Collins' loyal staff set to work preparing schemes to exploit our new acquisition to the full—but what none of us knew was that Mr Franklin, the Science Master, saw it as a golden opportunity to fulfil his lifelong ambition of firing a naval cannon. Already he was studying a book entitled *The History of Gunpowder,* together with *Naval Armaments Through the Ages,* both of which had been in his possession since boyhood.

TWO

While Mr Franklin measured and photographed the hardware on the gun-deck, Mr Tadd and Mr Figgin surveyed the ship's timbers with expert eyes. Chalk lines and symbols began to appear everywhere, trial borings were sunk and a great deal of technical language delighted the ear.

We learned that much defective timber must be sharked out, then shored up while new timber was scarfed in, spagged on, chuffed under, frogged to and butted up—not to mention continuous seaming, caulking, blistering, prouding, weathering and bleeding, plus some other phraseology of the trade quite pornographic out of context. According to Mr Tadd, much of the ship had been constructed from farmyard manure cunningly painted over to resemble wood, and he was fond of presenting handfuls of it to Dr Collins as proof. Dr Collins soon tired of receiving parts of the ship in a bucket and his visits rapidly lessened, especially when Mr Figgin showed him how to reduce a shackle-pin to powdered iron oxide with the aid of a four-pound hammer.

Whatever Dr Collins paused to inspect about the vessel, Mr Tadd took hold of it and crushed it to a fine powder-like dust or put his boot through it, always with the observation that it would have to be sharked out, shored up and scarfed in, then caulked and finally crapped down with a goose-bully.

"You'll also need eighty gallons of creosote for piddling up below the orlop deck, sir," Mr Tadd announced cheerfully, following his custom of breaking the news about expenses in easy stages each time the Head came aboard, and invariably phrasing his demands to let the Head know that he needed it, not Mr Tadd.

Dr Collins gasped and added this new item to his clipboard recording cubic feet of timber, clinchers, bleeders, froggits, male and female rapers, red lead, bastard reamers, sand blasters, left-handed crabs, split-maidens and many other essentials to marine repair. Dr Collins was appalled by the growing expense of this project, and rather embarrassed by Mr Tadd's trade terminology, so that he hid the list lest Mrs Collins should see it.

"I'll be hurrying back to school now, Mr Tadd," Dr Collins said, concealing the clip-board inside his briefcase.

"Just have a look at this gun-port before you go, sir." Mr Tadd wrenched part of the gun-port from the ship's side and handed it to the Head. "That's your death watch beetle, sir, and as you'll see from the plan there's nothing else supporting the quarter-deck over our heads except fresh air. Unless you trench out that port and spline in the new timber with metal shags the original spews will snout inwards under pressure and bring down the cuttles."

"Would that be bad, Mr Tadd?"

"Bad only in the sense that you and I would now be standing on the quarter-deck instead of the gun-deck and not speaking to each other."

"Have we quarrelled?"

"No, we've been crushed to death. Therefore you'll require a gross of steel shags, fifteen reinforced cuttles and a dozen extra strong spews—immediate delivery, I'd advise you."

Without another word Dr Collins added these new demands to his list and hurried ashore with a growing presentiment that he hated ships and those men who serviced them. He was determined to delegate store requisitioning to Mr Hamble, the Deputy Headmaster, that very day, directly he had taken the bath necessitated by visiting *Spirit of Adventure.* Dr Collins was so haunted by the question of where all the money was to come from that he failed to notice Mr Mould, who was boarding the ship in search of inspiration for his Religious Knowledge Scheme of Work.

Mr Mould often remarked how much easier his job would be

if he were teaching the Christian faith in Mecca, especially after his experience with Fred Rubble of 4G, Bible student extraordinary. At the moment Mr Mould was accompanied by our boy wonder, Crowhurst of 4A, having been unable to shake him off.

"Please, sir, do you believe in Transcendentalism?" Crowhurst inquired by way of small-talk.

"Yes," Mr Mould snapped shortly.

"I find it extremely difficult to understand, sir. Could you explain it to me?"

"No."

"Does it mean that God has a separate existence from the material universe, thus he is not bound by its physical limitations, sir?"

"Yes."

"Who first propounded such a concept, sir?"

"Probably you."

"Was it Schelling and Emerson, sir?"

"Yes."

"What is the second stage of Schelling's philosophy, sir?"

"That I, as God's agent, will strike you down in your tracks if you ask me one more question, Crowhurst. You must realize that since its inception in 1896 the Nobel Prize has never been awarded to a lad of fifteen, so your age is against you, boy. In any case why aren't you at games like normal children?"

"I'm excused games so I can research *Spirit of Adventure,* sir, and incorporate her in my project on the British Empire.

Can you explain the precise meaning of Pax Britannica for me, sir?"

"It was that glorious era of peace the world enjoyed until 1958."

"I thought it ended in 1914, sir."

"No, Crowhurst, 1958, the year you were born."

In his hand Mr Mould held a Bible, the one he had presented

to Fred Rubble to mark the breakthrough into Rubble's spiritual cement. Why, he asked himself, did this new convert request an old copy—one of the school's original stock rather than the latest edition? Why, he asked himself, did Rubble prefer the tiny print to today's bold type? Why, he asked himself, had so many pages of Genesis disappeared? Was he to accept Rubble's own explanation that in his zeal for the Gospel he tore out each page as he digested its contents?

Digested! Surely this revolting yob was not actually eating his way through the Old Testament? Was he mad enough to seek fame in the Guinness Book of Records as the first person to swallow a complete Bible? It was the deepest mystery of Mr Mould's long career in infant aberration, as he himself termed it.

"Have you ever encountered a case of ankylostomiasis, sir?"

"Not till I met you, Crowhurst."

"Hook-worm in the intestines must be extremely painful, sir."

"Yes, you are indeed."

"I mentioned it because it's part of my Biology project, sir."

"Shut up!"

"What I really wanted to ask you, sir, was your opinion of Doppler's Law."

"I detest it. Pubs should shut as late as they like. Furthermore, Crowhurst, rest assured I shall never cease in my efforts to have you transferred to Cudford Grammar School. Why you did not go there in the first place is beyond me."

"I'm a late developer, sir."

"Then within this enormous area of our school and playing fields will you kindly develop elsewhere? I am very busy."

"I expect you want to solve the mystery of Rubble's Bible, sir."

Mr Mould looked surprised. Surely this unprepossessing

youth with the buck teeth was not psychic as well as nauseating? "What do you know about the Bible, Crowhurst?" Mr Mould demanded.

"It consists of 39 Hebrew works in the Old Testament, 27 Greek works in the New Testament and 14 books of the Apocrypha, sir. The Bible contains 1,189 chapters, 31,173 verses and approximately or circa 774,680 words, sir. . . ."

"I mean this one in my hand, idiot!"

"Authorised Version, sir, James the First, 1611, not the Vulgate Bible by John Wycliffe, 1380, sir, nor the Revised . . ."

"I don't want to be told the history of everything from the year dot, man," Mr Mould shouted angrily. "All I need to know is why Rubble rips pages out of this book."

"Ah, that's different, sir. It could be a subconscious psychological protest against authority, sir. With great respect, sir, even against your good self."

"Listen, Crowhurst, all my prayers are directed above to secure divine protection from the two great evils of mankind— psychologists and you. If you don't know what Rubble is up to, give Providence a fair chance by going away."

"Follow me, sir, and perhaps I may be able to assist you."

Crowhurst led Mr Mould past Mr Tadd and Mr Figgin, who were hard at work in the Captain's dining-room aft. Mr Tadd did not look unlike a frigate under full canvas himself, with an impressive spread of mutton-chop whiskers flying well beyond the beam of his face. Mr Figgin, on the other hand, merely parked his hair out of the way on top of his head. They were sharking out the mahogany panelling from the room with expert hands, and one could not but notice how this mahogany panelling seemed to reappear later as the lining of Mr Tadd's cabin on his own yacht, so aptly named *Fancy Free*.

"We could do with Crowhurst on this job," Mr Tadd remarked. "I think he must be breaking those teeth in for a beaver."

"Gently steve your end fibbit clear of the chine, Bert, and she'll case free without damage," Mr Figgin calculated.

"Nice work, Sid. Just dove your mitre a fraction to me and she'll spring out a treat."

I could never understand how Messrs Tadd and Figgin chalked so many lines on the ship's side, yet were always taking timber from somewhere else. Nor could I fathom how Mr Figgin's cabin-cruiser *Pirate the Third,* was gradually acquiring a teak superstructure. It seemed nothing was beyond the capabilities of these two craftsmen, from furnace work to electronics. Last term a car had been abandoned in the school drive, but soon it was being dragged inside by our Fourth Year boys like ants round a dead wasp. Then we learned that Mr Figgin had begun a special engineering course for School Leavers, during which the car engine was stripped, reconditioned, converted to marine use and installed in *Pirate the Third.*

Simultaneously Mr Tadd introduced the boys to welding, enabling them to construct a yacht-trailer from a car chassis and Dunlop tyres which was exactly the correct size for towing behind Mr Tadd's Land Rover. Some of the boys were taught panel-beating, whereby they were able to turn the car's body into hatch-covers. Even the car's old-type AA badge found itself part of a sextant on *Fancy Free,* which now boasted windscreen-wipers.

Rumour had it that since Dr Collins introduced closed circuit television to the school, *Pirate the Third* had been equipped with radar and Mr Figgin had sailed to Spain during the sunmmer vacation, keeping in touch by radio with Mr Tadd, who was cruising down the Norwegian fiords. Another thing which vexed Dr Collins was that, although he could not prove it, the mast of *Fancy Free* had once flown the Union Jack above the school tower.

But Dr Collins' bitterest grievance concerned Neptune's trident in the quadrangle; the trident made of manganese-bronze; the trident made of non-corrosive manganese-bronze. When that metal was in short supply, Dr Collins observed Neptune still with his fist upraised to the sky but now grasping nothing. The trident had disappeared overnight. The Headmaster reported the loss to the police, but when Constable Barrington arrived with his notebook Neptune's fist now held a trident once more. Close examination revealed it to be a finely-made replica in iron, the shaft of which was stamped 'School Dinners Plate Rack. Front.'

Dr Collins was unable to get any further with his inquiries, though there were whispers about the staff room that, despite the national shortage of manganese-bronze, Mr Tadd had succeeded in casting a propeller from this rare metal. Dr Collins visited the school forge unit to check with Mr Tadd, only to discover Mr Tadd with his mutton-chop whiskers fully spread for character and atmosphere, beating out a horseshoe for Mrs Collins' own mare. When questioned about propellers Mr Tadd said Dr Collins was welcome to examine the propeller of *Fancy Free* as minutely as he wished, and that the school's shallow-water diving equipment was at his disposal day or night, with Mr Tadd personally standing by to operate the emergency resuscitation unit.

Crowhurst led Mr Mould down to the gun-deck, where some boys were rubbing down an ancient cannon so vigorously that smoke was rising from the barrel. In charge of the task was Fred Rubble, who was the only boy not rubbing, yet most of the smoke seemed to be rising from his immediate vicinity.

"It would be better if they didn't see me, sir," Crowhurst whispered behind the main capstan, "they might think I had grassed on them to you, sir."

"Surely they are not reckless enough to attempt firing a charge of gunpowder in that rusty piece of artillery, Crowhurst? Master Rubble, noteworthy example of the play-way to illiteracy, appears to be priming a fuse over the touchhole."

Mr Mould discovered he was addressing himself because Crowhurst had vanished as if by magic. He stared unbelievingly as Rubble lit the fuse, but instead of applying it to the gun's touch-hole he stuck it in his mouth until smoke issued from his nose. Then two other boys lit fuses and inserted them in their mouths, long white fuses covered with printed instructions. Boys actually smoking artillery fuses of a past age, Mr Mould gasped, like seamen had been known to drink the alcohol in a ship's compass. And the frigate the biggest fire hazard since wooden lighthouses.

How would the psychologists explain this lot? Mr Mould wondered—those clever gentlemen who strip us defenceless before a rising tide of violence, as he described them—Mr Mould would become extremely angry if they said Rubble had been taken from the breast of his mother too soon, so was now smoking an artillery fuse as compensation. Mr Mould resented any explanation whereby the remedy was fifteen years too late, just as he had told Dr Collins he was very sorry about the Negro problem in America, but that he personally had never shipped a single slave across the Atlantic and had had no hand in ill-treating them on the cotton plantations, any more than he had won the British Empire. Therefore he would take it most kindly if our Red friends would desist from calling him a White Imperialist and Oppressor of the Black Man, despite they themselves having amassed the largest imperialist empire the world had ever known as at 1973. He pointed out to Dr Collins that he still purchased Danish bacon irrespective of how the Danes had ravaged our country during the years A.D. 790 to 851, as a gesture of his magnanimity.

Mr Mould made no secret of the fact that he did not love psychologists as he should, if only because they had succeeded in making American children the more dreaded juveniles in history, and were now working on British children. Mr Mould had a daughter in the States who, according to him, was the mother of a miniaturized adult aged six, and when Mr Mould met the child for the first time he gained the impression he was holding in his arms a midget bootlegger intent on eliminating his grandfather from his territory.

"That's a lovely drag, in'it?" Rubble was observing in the Cudford patois. "I makes 'em just roight, don't I?"

"'Sorroight," Sandsod agreed. Sandsod was going through a difficult Artie phase, whereby he was obliged to paint his jeans various colours, presumably to let us know that true Art required him to spill a great deal of paint in the process. Hanging from a neck chain was a massive swastika, perhaps to remind us that Hitler painted too. Above the swastika was mostly hair, to us he was not a formal artist but a devotee of the modern school who favour the random splurge method rather than old-fashioned representational pictures which plague our art galleries still.

Sandsod had first discovered his talent the day of the country race, when he had volunteered to stay behind to re-decorate the art room with emulsion paint. When he had completed the ceiling, the art teacher, Mr Whittle, suggested he call it 'Krakatoa Erupts, 1833'. The four walls have been known ever since as 'The Conversion of St Paul on the Damascus Road'. and the door is celebrated as 'The Dying Gladiator', although Sandsod himself captioned it as "Wet Paint—Use Other Door'.

"Ain't arf strong," Groin exclaimed, doing his thing, as they say. Groin suffered ill-health in the shape of a diurnal allergy, whereby he was often unable to attend school by day, yet turn up to our discotheque—and P.T.A. bazaars by night. His mother explained to me how his chronic stomach upsets usually responded to treatment around 4 o'clock in the afternoon, enabling him to go out for fresh air and therapeutic dancing. Some of our girls also suffered from diurnal allergy, though for them an effective cure seemed to be shopping.

"All we wants now is a pint, in'it?" Rubble reflected, leaning on the cannon in pub bar fashion. Rubble was a man of the world, being taken to Spain on holiday by his parents twice a year, once during the spring term and once during the summer vacation—yet he qualified for free school meals. Each Monday he drew his five free tokens, sold them to other children at 12p each, then ate sandwiches in his dad's Zephyr parked near the gates, so he could listen to the radio. The Zephyr was parked near the gates because Mr Rubble could no longer stand up to the rat-race of modern industry, which required him to get up and go to work before the pubs were even open. A victim of the industrial society, Mr Rubble now lay in his bed a broken man, struggling to recoup sufficient strength to seek a little human company in the Bold Forester each midday and evening, where spiritual uplift emerged from a pump and physical rehabilitation was encouraged by darts. Here Mr Rubble was permitted to purge his soul of bitterness against a system which forced him to exist on the very margin of survival unless he toiled in the sweat-shops of the rich capitalists of Cudford on a pittance of forty pounds a week. Mr Rubble often expressed a desire to introduce Communism to Britain, though it was difficult to see where he himself would fit into the system. Mr Mould put it down to a death wish on Mr Rubble's part, and suggested that the Rubble family should emigrate to Russia in order to cause the collapse of the regime.

Unable to contain his wrath any longer, Mr Mould emerged from behind the main capstan. "Come here, wretched youth!" he roared at Rubble.

"It's old Moses!" Rubble cried, using Mr Mould's professional title. The great Patriarch snatched the fuse from the boy's lips, twirling the end between finger and thumb to extinguish it. As he did so he was amazed to read the word *Genesis* on the instructions, and to discover the content was not gunpowder but tobacco.

"Cigarettes!" he stormed. "Rolled in pages ripped from my Bible. No wonder you wanted an old copy, you vile yob—rice paper!"

"Them new books won't keep alight, sir. . . ."

"Silence, you obnoxious Philistine."

"What's going on down here?" It was Mr Tadd, brought to the scene by the shouting.

"This hirsute vandal is rolling cigarettes from my Bible pages and smoking them in the confines of this floating bonfire they call a ship, Mr Tadd."

"Disgraceful," Mr Tadd observed, puffing his pipe with indignation. "If there's once thing I cannot tolerate it is misuse of school property, not to mention smoking and creating a fire hazard."

"But you're smoking too, sir," Rubble pointed out.

"What an observant young man, to be sure," Mr Tadd purred, caressing Rubble's curls with the mallet he carried, and when you reach my age you too will be permitted to indulge in a pipe whilst you slave away to help the rising generation."

Rubble found himself in a position of unaccustomed perplexity, wondering if it would be wise to mention the other similarity between him and Mr Tadd apropos the misuse of school property, with special reference to his youthful agility in scaling Neptune for the purpose of changing tridents in mid-air. He deemed it the lesser evil to say nothing.

"I suggest you leave these three lads with me for appropriate punishment, Mr Mould, rather than expose them to the savagery of our Headmaster," Mr Tadd suggested, smiling esoterically.

"An excellent idea, Tadd. I do not wish the Head to accuse me of seeking revenge on a helpless child who has not yet learned to distinguish between right and wrong, nor to be asked what is right and what is wrong, nor to be committed before a psychologist in order to be taught how there are no such attributes as good or evil, and that the difference between sanity and insanity is of our own making, so it is I who am insane as a consequence of my unnatural conditioning as a child by parents who ruled me by fear and sexual frustration . . ."

"Just leave the whole business to me, Mr Mould."

"Nor do I wish to be arraigned before some senile magistrate to be charged, in the cloistered atmosphere of effete law, as the monster who clipped the boy's ear in a fit of power-drunk sadism; struck a defenceless victim whose only other offence was that last year, on the whim of sudden impulse, he did rifle some twenty-seven gas-meters in this area over a period of three months . . ."

"Yes, yes, Mr Mould, calm yourself, please. I will handle the disciplinary side of it."

"Much better that you do, Tadd. I should not like it on my conscience that these poor lads were exposed to our Head-master's lashing tongue as he told them they were naughty boys and must not do it again or he might have to keep them in after school—No, sir, I abhor the probability of their young personalities being warped for life by such harsh words, and the possibility of their taking to crime because we crush their emergent ethos under the weapon of fear . . ."

"Don't worry, Mr Mould, I believe in instant psychology," Mr Tadd butted in, holding the mallet over Rubble's head. "My patient rubs his head, saying puzzledly 'Why is there a bruise on my head?' Then he starts thinking. 'Ah, I know; it was hit with a mallet. Now why was it hit with a mallet? Ah, I know; I tore pages from Bibles'. Then the association of ideas takes place, thus: The patient says 'Ah, here is another Bible, but if I tear pages out a big lump will come up on my head. I do not think I will tear these pages out even for fag papers'."

Mr Mould held up his hands aghast. "Pray, Mr Tadd, do not contemplate striking the boy's head. Popular myth has it that Master Rubble harbours a vestigial brain therein, though in my opinion any such organ must be situated in his trousers. As proof I quote from his last essay on Christian Aid: 'Fire, fire!' screamed the old lady from the burning building, so the sheriff took careful aim before firing and shot her through the heart'."

"I was only joking, Mr Mould, despite the fact that people are nightly coshed, shot, maimed and worse on television. I have ascertained that Sandsod here watches up to fifty hours of television every week. As the experts assure us there is no evidence to suppose television influences us, we can be pretty certain that it does, especially as the advertisers are willing to pay thousands of pounds for a 30-second flash. I first began to mistrust experts when I used to back horses."

"An expert is a specialist in his subject who possesses an uncanny gift of hindsight," Mr Mould mused. "Of course, my own humble opinions are based merely on experience and common sense, therefore quite valueless. For example, I do not require a £20,000 grant for a two-year project to discover whether children like sweets or not. Nevertheless, when I observe what is euphemistically called a pop superstar dressed or undressed—as an Ancient Briton and appropriately woaded up with facial dye in order to shout a jungle fertility chant to the effect that—and I quote—we ain't got no morals so let's bust up our schools and so on, I sometimes wonder where we are heading."

"I think one of the great dangers of television is the way it persuades us to watch life rather than live it ourselves, turning us into voyeurs as we see highly-paid professionals having a vicarious party on our behalf at New Year's Eve. In our darkened rooms we watch them eating for us, drinking for us, dancing for us, cracking jokes for us, singing for us, kissing for us even welcoming in the New Year for us. This to me is bordering on the macabre—half the nation sitting as silent, passive spectators of their own party, relying on actors to laugh for them and produce some kind of secondhand enjoyment. Surely we are not to be relegated to Peeping Toms spying on life?"

Rubble often heard this kind of conversation between Mr Mould and Mr Tadd. Normally he did not listen to it, let alone understand it; all he knew was that such dialogues were not pro-Rubble dialogues—in fact, they were often extremely anti-Rubble. He had learned from experience that topics like the Common Market, Vietnam and teachers' pay scales—even Mr Mold's wife—were definitely not pro-Rubble topics because they often led to his being punished for things he had not done, such as his homework, or things he had done, such as damaging his own toilets at the school.

Dr Collins provided very decent toilets for the pupils, but Rubble and Co had a strange attitude to toilets, smashing the minors and removing the taps and stealing the chain—until eventually they had no toilets to use. Yet the lads set great store by the school. It was the focal point of their world, and often they had nothing else, certainly little home life. It was a complete mystery; more so because even Rubble and Co did not seem to know why they did it, and Mr Mould considered they were not intelligent enough to be masochists. Our school psychiatrist suggested it might be the boy's subconscious protest against society, whereupon Mr Mould called him a shocking double-barrelled name I had not heard since I was in the Navy.

When Mr Mould had departed, Mr Tadd gently brushed Rubble's hair with the mallet, like a ladies' hairdresser, and said, "Listen, lads, you're old enough now for me to teach you one of life's most important lessons. Crime doesn't pay for the likes of you because you're so thick that you get nabbed first time out—give it up. The jails are packed with lads like you who couldn't do a shop over even if the police were on strike or promised not to look. In fact, Fred, if ever there's a big crime committed in your manor you'd best nip round smartly to the police station and give yourself up so as to establish some sort of alibi the moment you hear of it."

Rubble looked extremely crestfallen, listening to his failure as a master-criminal. He knew it was true because last year he had assisted his elder brother Steve to commit what Constable Barrington dubbed in court as the perfect crime. Three tiny clues gave them away. First, Steve failed to open the office safe because it was so old-fashioned, and, second, he cut his hand in the attempt, which bled profusely. But worst of all, the getaway van would not start because Fred forgot to get petrol. As the van belonged to Steve they had to push it through Cudford at three in the morning, followed by an inquisitive dog smelling blood and awakening the town with its barking—so loudly persistent that Constable Barrington emerged from the police station as the van went by, to discover the van was neither taxed nor insured for the carriage of housebreaking implements lying in the back. Also he found that the front tyres were worn beyond the permitted limit and the windscreen-wipers did not function. Lastly, Steve was unable to produce a current driving-licence. After Steve's hand had been stitched up at Cudford Infirmary he made a voluntary statement to Constable Barrington to the effect that he and his brother had been pushing the van round to Rumbold's Garage in order to obtain an M.O.T. certificate and they wanted to be first in the morning queue, to which Constable Barrington smiled sympathetically and said what a pity it was that Rumbold's did not open on Sundays, so they could just as well have left the van at the scene of the crime and gone home to bed.

"I am the large, nasty teacher you refer to privately as Tadpole," Mr Tadd continued, preening his whiskers.

"But you're one of the teachers I likes," Rubble confessed.

"Oh, cruel youth—the unkindest cut of all. Conceal this hideous predilection from the staff or I am lost."

Despite his rough manner Mr Tadd was extremely popular with the boys, who instinctively admired any teacher who was firm in discipline and a master of his trade.

"Now, Rubble and Co, because you have learned already to keep your big fat mouths shut about matters which do not concern you, such as my advanced methods of trident technology, I shall not punish you this time."

"Oh, thank you, sir."

"Rather shall I reward you."

"Oh, thank you, sir."

"I shall permit you to carry the defective panels which Mr Figgin and I are working on in the Captain's dining-room across to the *Fancy Free,* that they may be treated for woodworm.

"Oh!"

"Do not say Oh! like that in response to such a singular honour I have bestowed upon you, boy. Get mobile before I mallet the three of you."

Woodwork and Metalwork were Rubble's favourite subjects, so he often did well in them and was suitably rewarded by Mr Tadd, who let him clear up the workshop after school. But if he did wrong, neither Mr Tadd or Mr Figgin ever punished him, but rewarded him by letting him clear up the workshop after school. He found it all rather confusing, being rewarded whether he did right or wrong. Mr Tadd often explained to him that boys will be boys, and should not be punished for robust horseplay, as he phrased it. Rather they should be permitted to experience success and reward, which was why Rubble was a favourite pupil and allowed the privilege of setting up the workshops before school, cleaning out the forge and clearing up at the end of the day.

"You're the only teacher what ain't never punished me, sir," Rubble told Mr Tadd admiringly.

"No doubt your English teacher has good reason to, Rubble, if you address him with a broadside of double negatives, but for my part I abhor the very mention of punishment in modern education, relying entirely on the motivation of reward. That is why you and your two chums are permitted to run my workshops yourselves. After school today, when you have cleared up the Rough Unit and the workshops I intend showing you how to rub down a clinker-built dinghy."

"But we ain't got no dinghy, sir ."

"We ain't got no dinghy here, Rubble, but there is one on the *Fancy Free.*"

"Oh, thank you, sir."

"After which, if your conduct is exemplary, I shall entrust you with the skilled art of painting it with primer, undercoat, topcoat and varnish."

"Cor! Ain't we lucky!"

"Think yourself fortunate indeed, boy, that you receive your education from such an enlightened tutor as myself. Now proceed at once to Mr Figgin, who also wishes to reward you for your commendable seamanship in holystoning the deck of *Pirate the Third.*"

"Two best teachers in the school," Rubble remarked to Sandsod and Groin as they hurried off for more praise and prizes.

THREE

I discovered very early on that the good folks of Cudford Council Estate, whatever their politics, were the most conservative and class-conscious people I had ever met. My friends who predicted I should find myself in the hub of the permissive society where I should be torn to pieces mentally and physically must have received such a false picture from television and the press. On the contrary, the majority living here were what we may call old-fashioned—even prim—by modern standards, and this I liked.

Their pre-war attitudes were reflected in their offspring, and it often occurred to me that if ever Britain is to lose class distinctions, here are the people who will be the hardest to convert. The ceaseless propaganda of the popular media beat against them in vain to become hedonists and irreligious. Basically, Cudford Council Estate was a matriarchal society, ruled by two excellent goddesses I came to know as Mum and Nan. Dad did not come out of it too well, being the weaker Partner of marriage who all too often tended to disappear when the children were young, or otherwise opt out of his responsibilities—sometimes to be replaced by a gentleman I came to know as Uncle.

We had little serious trouble at Cudford School, but what did arise was so often traceable back to the missing or inadequate Dad. Of course, there were exceptions to the rule, where Mum had gone and so Dad was bringing up the children admirably; or where both parents had gone, leaving the job to Nan, but on the whole our pupils enjoyed the advantages of a happy home life provided by two good parents.

Nevertheless, I quickly discovered that to many of the less fortunate children I was a Dad figure—some actually called me Dad occasionally—children badly in need of affection, interest, praise and, above all, a feeling of security and stability. These youngsters, so affectionate towards me, were not so to each other, being peevish and aggressive. There was constant niggling, pinching, punching and backbiting amongst them, so that without a teacher present the classroom rapidly became a riot. Two or three, including a girl, possessed the sudden and unexpected habit of kicking each other in the groin.

They were labelled remedial children, whom I found dffficult to teach for the reason that their low ability was so restricting, and their unstable dispositions made it hard for them to wait for anything—like Christmas, when Sandra gave me a Christmas card on 30th November and Julie was wearing her jewellery presents a week later. Nor were the majority of them deprived financially, as I had been led to expect despite Mr Mould's observation of our modern paradox where the poor earn more than the rich. They were well dressed, had such luxuries as transistor radios—and Susan's father gave her £10 for Easter.

I learned to gallop out of the classroom in the wake of Kenneth, toilet-roll at the ready, in order to unlock the lavatory for his immediate use. I learned that Valerie must take her tablets on the hour by my watch lest she drop dead at my feet. I learned to clear the room if Barry had a fit on the floor, but not to touch him. I learned that Keith was liable to throw up at any moment during my discourse, but that he had the presence of mind to open his desk at the critical second for the operation, then cheerfully carry the desk downstairs to wash it out.

To help me introduce the Queen's English to our two remedial forms Dr Collins had appointed a Miss Dewar. I thought at first her name was Miss Doooor until she explained, "It's the same as the famous wusky the Scots drink at footba' matches—Doooor. But I'd be awfa' pleased if you'd call me by ma first name, Karrrrn."

"What is your first name, Miss Doooor?"

"Karrrm Doooor. I'll wreet it doon for you."

As she wrote Karen Dewar on the blackboard I panicked

badly, excusing myself and fleeing to the staff toilet. Glancing in the mirror I did not like what I saw. It was my face but all too visible were the telltale beads of sweat running down the narrow channel separating my eyes. Using the faucet I swallowed two of my tablets I always carried in case of an attack, then pulled out the pocket manual issued by *Retreat* and began to read the chapter headed 'When, Where and How to Hide'.

Retreat was a kind of Men's Lib organization I joined last year just to be on the safe side. You may recall from my novels that there was a time when I displayed a passing interest in the fair sex, which was now all over and done with, thanks to *Retreat*. Nowadays I looked upon my fellow men in the staff room with almost mocking contempt as they ogled the women teachers, rather like a man who has given up smoking right through January 1st and despises those still hooked on the disgusting habit.

You may also recall how, if I had a weakness at all, it was for the Scots lassies, but now even those northern charmers left me cold—although I had been disturbed to discover that the HR rating on my *Retreat* membership card stood for High Risk, which meant I still had to carry the tablets on my person.

Retreat held the view that because men were not strong enough to resist women our only salvation was to retreat—which was actually the bugle call of our organization—or, in the graphic language of the manual, beat it. Having retreated, we then had to hide, while we recovered our wits and regrouped. This was the basic principle devised by our President in London, though his whereabouts were not publicized because he himself was often in hiding. He admitted we might find the strategy somewhat humiliating at first, but, as he pointed out, every other method had failed miserably so this was our last hope.

What worried me about Karen Dewar was not so much the singsong dialect but her eyes. I had never believed the poet's guff about eyes sparkling and laughing, any more than other organs like cars could sparkle and laugh—but now I had just seen it happen. I looked in the mirror again to check on my own eyes, and as usual I saw the dead stare of blue glass framed with red veins, so I figured Karen's black sparklers had been a figment of my imagination. I laughed derisively into the mirror at my cold strong reflection and hoped my adamant personality would not break the poor girl's heart. I also figured to ask Dr Collins if she could be replaced by Miss Ross, elderly spinster dubbed by Mr Mould as Women's Revenge. Owing to his wife, Mr Mould did not have a high opinion of the ladies, advising me that if it were not for perpetuating the species we should not even speak to them, with special reference to H.M.S. *Warspite* whom he had wed in mistake for a wife.

It was not that I had any qualms about Miss Dewar now I was a confirmed misogynist, Scots or not, but I had already paid a total of £21 in fines to *Retreat* and my membership card had been endorsed HR upon the sixth fine, so I did not want any risk of misunderstanding or gossip. As our President stressed so often, all our energies must be channelled into creative production, not dissipated in sex. I still smarted under the penalty of having my photograph published in the August number of *Retreat,* and, worse still, having members write in to inquire how I had managed to woman-proof my face and why didn't it work. One wretch went so far as to ask if I had been involved in the current air crash, and I also received literature from an American plastic surgery enterprise offering me a rebuild job with payment spread over twenty years. Actually I had been a beautiful child until my prowess at boxing and football—especially rugby—had slightly blemished my good looks by flattening the nose and moving the lips rather too far to the left for perfect symmetry. Unfortunately this was accentuated by a tiny scar joining the corner of my mouth to the left eye, recording the passage of a Welsh boot in the act of scoring its fiftieth point at half-time.

My confidence slowly returned as I chanted the stabilizer formula—'It's All in the Mind'—one hundred times, though personally I did not consider this the best of chants because for me that was just about the worst place to have it. I returned to Miss Dewar, my face a façade of cold marble to let her see I was not just a woman's plaything but a kind of didactic monk under a vow of chastity.

"How air yew faring with the Remedials, Peter?" she crooned in Scottish ballad tone.

"Awful. I've had to abandon the recommended play-way to learning. Any suggestion of a game to this mob and it's like Rangers versus Celtic at Hogmanay," I replied, employing the Scottish analogy to account for my classroom being wrecked.

What made it so difficult to control Remedials was the fact that they were not sufficiently intelligent to realize you had gone berserk in public, because they thought this was normal adult behaviour and thoroughly enjoyed it. If you acted quietly they considered you were ill, so ignored you completely.

"Have you tried," she whispered, "old-fashioned repetition work from a text-book?"

I glanced round guiltily in case we were overheard. "Repetition work from a text-book!" I exclaimed.

"Yes, and things like spelling tests, Peter. The kids love them."

"You must be mad, Miss Dewar." I had still not recovered from Poetry during my Teaching Practice, when the College Lecturer had reprimanded me for analysing the structure and devices of Poetry with an examination class. "Poetry is to be enjoyed, not dissected like a dead rat—not even for examination purposes," he had informed me coldly, thus leaving me with no material for a six-weeks' course with a class who were determined not to enjoy Poetry however it was presented. It was like sending a juggler on the stage, then confiscating his balls.

"Try it just once, Peter," Miss Dewar begged. "No one need

know, I promise. And I do wish you'd call me Karrrrn instead of Miss Doooor—please?"

I did not answer because I was experiencing trouble with my iron will. Not even a celibate like mys :lf should be put to such a test, especially as the next fine would be £7 and a severe reprimand recorded on vellum, plus being gazetted in *Retreat* as a drop-out. Apart from one's mother and other close female relations, members are not permitted to address girls except in cases of necessity, like if they are drowning; thus it was extremely difficult for me to work alongside Miss Dewar with the black hair, glen-to-glen voice and Highland Fling eyes without some trace of emotion. Through slitted lids I noticed also that she possessed the Ben Nevis figure of Inverness-shire, so, mustering all my dignity I strode past her without a word and disappeared into the Gents. Was all that counselling and cathartic callisthenics in vain, that my steely resolve should be affected by this female person from porridge-land? I felt ashamed in the knowledge that the last five fines were the result of Scottish lassies taking advantage of my English sophistication, in that I was ill-equipped to withstand witchcraft disguised as friendship, and I was under direct orders from the President of *Retreat* that I was not to so much as sing *Auld Lang Syne* in public.

Henceforth I was so jumpy about Miss Dewar that I would not even follow her advice re Remedials lest it be contaminated. I resolved to try the Outward Looking approach instead, by inviting two experts in their fields to address the pupils, The first gentleman was a Trade Union official of long standing who spoke about the role of the Unions in helping the children when they started work. The second speaker was a retired army General of the old school who talked about the Army as a possible career.

Next day I quizzed the form for reactions, scanning the rows of Julies, Susans, Stephens and Ians—the trend names of the day—and this is exactly what happened.

"Now, class, who's going to tell me about the expert gentleman from the Trade Unions?" I inquired sternly, lest there should be any hint of another learning game in my voice.

"He's dinnie, sir," one of the Julies replied.

"In what way did you find him dinnie, Julie?" The chief aim of this question was to find out what dinnie meant.

"Well, sir, he was so sort of boring like."

"Many important things in life sometimes seem boring, but didn't you learn a lot about starting work when you leave school?"

"I couldn't understand nuffing what 'e said," a Stephen volunteered.

"My Dad won't join a Union," Ian the Third observed shortly.

"He was more sort of boring than the teachers, in'e?"

"If 'e comes again I'll skive off."

Dismayed by their reaction I thought it best to dispose of the General as quickly as possible, whose prewar Oxford accent had made the class titter at the beginning of the talk.

"Oh, he was lovely, sir," Susan enthused, "and he patted me on the 'ead."

"Don't 'e talk posh, sir? Can we have him again?"

"I finks I'll join the Army and be a General like."

"I wish 'e was my Dad."

"Can't we 'ave proper lessons like the other classes, sir?"

Once more I reeled at the way practice so often turns out very different from theory. "What do you mean by proper lessons, Stephen?"

"Well, roightin' in books wiv a pen, sort of."

Out of the mouths of babes and sucklings! Without more ado I determined to inaugurate proper lessons. I began where nobody could accuse me of overreaching myself or racking their brains, by exhorting the class to copy out a page from a simple text-book, neatly and without errors. They took to this at once, and I was soon to learn an important lesson myself—that any school work not connected with writing in an exercise-book, preferably in conjunction with a text-book, was a fraud on the part of the teacher and a sign of his incompetence or laziness; a view held inviolate by parents as well as pupils. Any other methods—such as outside visits or television lessons—were considered a waste of time and money, being merely unnecessary repetitions of what the children did in their spare time anyway.

Another lesson I learned was that in this modern age the teacher is hard put to compete with the sophisticated mass media when he uses such visual aids as slides, pictures and models. For example, children accustomed to seeing men walking on the moon, or queen bees laying eggs inside the hive—all in colour—were little impressed by my slides of Cudford Canal, so blurred and indistinct on the classroom wall that I felt like a Caveman showing his flint axe to the crew of a Polaris submarine. In fact, I grew to dread the familiar cry in the classroom of "I seen all this on telly!" I was forced to the conclusion that today the teacher does best when he sticks to his own field of tuition, inculcating concentration, accuracy and basic skills.

Before I could do anything with the Remedials I had to teach them elementary concentration on the job they were doing, for their lack of self-discipline precluded concentration, with the result they could accomplish almost nothing. In desperation I rearranged the desks so they sat alone instead of in groups. This cut down the petty pinching, niggling and chatting—even fighting—which was death to progress. Eventually I managed to introduce them to silence while they tackled their work independently, without aid or hindrance from their neighbours.

Next, I experimented with little spelling tests, comprehension exercises and simple word manipulation—even poetry. Un-expectedly again, they liked the discipline of my room and appeared to enjoy the work. I set great store upon neatness and accuracy—some children could only attain to these in their search for success—praised lavishly and marked generously. They seemed proud to be doing Proper Work from books, and undoubtedly they liked the new atmosphere of peaceful industry. Michael and Andrew nearly drove me off my rocker by insisting I mark their books at the end of every line. They were merely copying out poetry but it was vital that each line should be checked by me for accuracy and neatness; that is to say, every thirty seconds, whereupon they registered academic bliss.

Stephen the Third could write quickly, so he wanted marking only at the completion of each page, always with the same observation that "I'm a clever boy, ain't I, sir? Can I 'ave A?"

I duly recorded 'A' at the bottom of each page in the guilty knowledge that I had so motivated this lad that he was literally copying out the entire novel of *Robinson Crusoe*. Moreover, he was taking it home to do at night, proud to have homework. Remedials were never set homework, chiefly because we could never get our books back, so this was a special privilege for Stephen—as I constantly emphasized and each morning he returned with another chunk of *Robinson Crusoe* to be marked and awarded 'A'.

Sometimes his exercise-book would be muddy from its travels, or *Robinson Crusoe* would be dog-chewed or little-brother ripped, all of which he explained in his flat voice while I religiously waded through this accursed saga of island life I had once loved. One day *Robinson Crusoe* had a small hole right through the middle, just large enough to pass a pencil through, as Stephen proved by demonstration like a conjuring act. From now on there was always a word missing from his homework book, carefully circled with an ink line and labelled 'Hole in Page'—although occasionally a footnote would inform me that 'My little sister tore this page out and give it to our dog. She is 5'. Another footnote told me that 'I ain't dun no homework tonight because they cut the light off'.

So impressed had Stephen been by my plea for neatness that any blotches were ringed round and labelled 'Soup (Heinz)'. or 'Grotty old pen'. Once I discovered a smudge whose doggy origin I should have preferred not to know. Another idiosyncrasy of Stephen's was to write P.T.O. at the bottom of each page in case I didn't know what to do at that stage, and when he encountered the word musick he noted 'I think Robinson Crusoe has made a spelling mistake, not me.' Largely to get Stephen off *Robinson Crusoe,* and Michael and Andrew off *Verse for the Young,* I initiated the class into the mysteries of yet another incredibly boring chore I named Vocabulary. Like many of my lessons this one stemmed from the books available to me, in this case nearly a hundred dictionaries. One of the secrets of education, I discovered, was to ascertain what books lay in the stock-cupboard, choose one which made up a set of at least thirty, then base your lessons on it. I called this Pook's First Law of Survival—its corollary stated that lessons based on fifteen copies were hell, and lessons based on a sole copy were impossible.

I gave each boy a dictionary—I say boy because mostly the girls were absent or had unofficially left school for various reasons connected with not coming to school—and taught the class how to find a word before they too left school. Apart from Michael who didn't believe a dictionary could be alphabetical and looked up every word by starting at A, and took a week to locate Zebra, the class were fascinated by this miracle of classification. We played a game to see who could find Ant first, then Bee, then Cat, then we stopped playing the game before somebody got injured.

While Michael searched for Ant I showed the others how to find a word quickly, then write it down together with its definition. They tackled the task with unaccustomed zest.

"Please, sir, I've found Ant," Michael cried triumphantly,

his finger stabbing Ant for proof.

"Good lad. Enter it in your exercise-book, plus what it means." I was too weary to argue.

Michael rested his left ear on the desk, then painstakingly moved lips and pen simultaneously to record: 'Ant—back end of ship'.

"Please, sir, will you mark my work?" he demanded. I obliged in thoughtful mood, then assigned him to Bee in the hope he would not define it as something we sleep on. He avoided this trap, defining it as 'A wager or gamble'.

But Michael did slowly improve, as he must after five weeks of unremitting Vocabulary wherein I personally reached saturation point, yet the children were hooked on it as if I had given them drugs. In the stock-cupboard I unearthed an ancient relic of Early Education, called *Look It Up,* (Revised 1918, 1946), in a dusty stack of thirty copies. The Introduction informed us that its purpose was to provide practice for the pupil in the vital art of using a dictionary, thus: 'Does a lamplighter EXTINGUISH the gaslamps in our streets each evening? Look up the word EXTINGUISH in your dictionary. It means To Put Out. Answer:—No, a lamplighter does not EXTINGUISH the gaslamps in our streets each evening. He LIGHTS them'.

Obviously *Look It Up* had been written for me, more so because following the above example were One Thousand Questions for You to Look Up in Your Dictionary.

With supreme difficulty I weaned the class from Vocabulary to *Look It Up,* but directly they comprehended it was almost the same they took it to their hearts like tobacco. Several boys were now taking the books home to do at night, and other teachers complained to me that Andrew, Michael, Ian and Stephen were doing *Look It Up* during their own lessons. Stephen declared that not only was English his favourite subject but that I was the bestest teacher he'd ever had in his whole life. During the second half of man's nearest approach to eternity, the double period, I had let them play chess, but now the chess boards lay idle as my dictionaries were gradually worn out with ceaseless thumbing as they toiled under the ruthless domination of *Look It Up*.

Stephen told me in confidence that his Dad was also doing it under cover of night, now he was out of jail and couldn't obtain another telly, from which I deduced that *Look It Up* was even reducing the crime rate in our area.

"Any bother with the Remedials, Pook?" Dr Collins inquired in the safety of the staff room.

"Pretty well under control, sir."

"That's the ticket, Pook. Plenty of Free Expression and Practical Work for the non-academic streams. Let them get out and about to see, feel, touch, hear and smell the world around them. Widen their horizons and give them new experiences, draw them out with Drama and Song, stimulate their awareness with Music, turn their inarticulate ideas into Dance, titillate their imaginations with Literature, show them the clouds, let them smell the flowers and touch the wet sod."

"Exactly, sir." Pook's Law Number Two: Agree with everybody, especially with those who don't have to do it.

"Between you and me, Pook, I'm a trifle concerned about our Miss Dewar."

"Me too, sir."

"I thought you would be, Pook, because, unlike yourself, she tends to be different to the rest of the staff."

"Scottish, sir."

"No, I mean she would appear to favour old-fashioned methods of teaching, which can be particularly damaging to Remedials."

"Disgraceful, sir."

"She may be undoing a lot of your own good work."

"I sense that already, sir. I wish you would replace her by Miss Ross—I'd feel much safer."

"She is, of course, a most attractive young lady, Pook."

"To me she is just another mistress, sir. But she is Formal instead of Progressive, so must go. There is also the danger that the Remedials may soon be speaking Scots, sir, instead of the Queen's English. Only yesterday Stephen asked me why you wear a black goon in school and was it to keep your wee suitie clean." Pook's Law Number Three: Always make the Head's affairs the focal point of any discussion with him, thus putting him on the defensive.

"Dear me, an unforeseen hazard. I must indeed give the matter considerable thought, Pook."

"And arrive at the best solution for all parties, sir, as usual. Your sagacious judgement will spare us the embarrassment of Remedials being further retarded by out-dated formal lessons instead of the play-way to success. However, sir, should you in your wisdom decide that I should give up Remedials instead to spare Miss Dewar's feelings I shall naturally abide by your decision." Pook's Law Number Four: Plant the seed early and persistently.

Unfortunately Miss Ross produced a letter from her medical adviser insisting that her return to Remedial work might lead to a state of mind known in the teaching profession as going off your rocker—which in Miss Ross's case might be but a short journey. Poor Miss Ross tackled teaching like a marathon runner with a wooden leg who has lost the course, yet she battled on gamely in a school much too tough for her.

"I trust you are making good use of my own humble textbook, *English is Fun?*" Dr Collins plugged. "Though I say it myself, that little volume contains the true spirit of education."

You could often smell the true spirit of education when talking to Dr Collins because he kept it bottled in his office desk, in a drawer labelled 'Duke of Edinburgh Award Scheme', being a martyr to bronchitis.

"I use it constantly, sir," I replied truthfully. At this very moment it was serving to prevent my bookcase wobbling. *English is Fun* consisted of a complete course based on adventures like the burning down of the Crystal Palace and travelling to America by zeppelin, so far ahead of its time that Dr Collins had never revised it. Mr Mould had suggested it should now be transferred to the History Department.

Dr Collins smiled with pleasure. "Ah, Peter, you should go far in our profession. I need hardly ask if you are taking full advantage of our gallant frigate in your lessons. You see, to justify the considerable and unexpected expenditure involved, she must be exploited to the utmost."

"Indeed, sir. Like most of the staff I am getting all I can out of her."

Though not so much as the indefatigable Mr Tadd, who, moustachios and beard schooner-rigged so that in profile he resembled a bush sculptured by a topiarian gardener, was already laying down the keel of *Fancy Free the Second,* in which he hoped to be the first man to cross the Atlantic without cost or sponsor. To this end our Technical Drawing Department's pupils were hard at work planning what he called The Tadd Fartmaster Propulsion Unit, a power-plant dispensing with propellers and based on the toy boat driven by underwater jets of hot air.

"Don't underrate the complexity of the task, Pook," he told me as I assisted him carry to the workshops on a trolley the fifth discarded classroom heater from the caretaker's shed for cannibalization. "Before the war Woolworths used to sell a clever little boat for sixpence, called a putt-putt driven by the expulsion of air heated by a meth tablet, but to construct a full-size power-plant on the same principle requires ingenuity."

I was extremcely impressed. "But surely you don't intend crossing the Atlantic on methylated spirit, Mr Tadd?"

"Too dangerous and expensive, Peter. By what I term inventor's luck it has transpired by calculation that peak engine efficiency can be obtained only by using common domestic fuel oil such as is supplied to fire the admirable central-heating system recently installed in our school."

"What a lucky coincidence, Mr Tadd!"

"Invention has its rewards as well as heart-breaks, Peter. Remember the ancient hymn we often sing at Assembly—'With a glad and fulsome mind, Praise the Head for he is kind,'? How fortunate we are to serve under such a benefactor to science."

At that moment the benefactor himself appeared at our side as if by magic, a slight odour of bronchitis in the air and eyes large with classroom heaters on trolleys. "Where on earth are you transporting that old heater, Mr Tadd?" he inquired in his security patrol voice.

Mr Tadd plumed his facial sails. "Helping the caretaker find some space in his shed, sir. So where better to take scrap metal than to the Metalwork Department to eke out our annual capitation, ha, ha, ha, ha!"

"I see. By the way, how is work progressing on our frigate?"

"Excellently, sir. Rest assured that Mr Figgin and I are stripping her out as fast as is humanly possible. As you well know, there is not a Department in the land who can strip out as speedily as ours—in fact, both Mr Figgin and myself have been working on her in the evenings with the help of some of the less able lads. Keeps them off the streets and out of mischief, sir."

"But how far must she be stripped down before she can be built up, Mr Tadd?" Dr Collins asked puzzledly, his nightmare being to visit the berth and find it empty but surrounded by yachts.

"Take my word, sir, she'll be stripped out completely by the end of the summer term because Mr Figgin and I are sailing to America during the holidays."

"To America! In the *Spirit of Adventure?*"

"No, sir, in *Fancy Free the Second,* my new oil-driven

cruiser now on the keel-blocks next to *Pirate the Third.*"

Dr Collins wondered if that fantastic story about Mr Tadd which still persisted in the staff room could be true,concerning the great post-war nylons scandal. Yet how else could all other Allied prisoners had been released when the war ended in 1945? and where did Mr Figgin fit into the mystery?

Briefly, the story centred round a small Army Vehicle Maintenance Depot situated in the British Sector of Berlin where Mr Tadd was serving. There was one small store, little bigger than a lock-up garage, which contained 100,000 pairs of nylon stockings, though some observers said it contained 100,000 packets each holding one dozen pairs, so tightly packed in that the consignment was the exact shape of the store. Mr Tadd merely wished to relieve the acute shortage of nylons among the ladies, so in order to allay suspicion—as he thought at the time—he would ration each lady to twelve pairs. He discreetly advertised the offer by word of mouth but even he was surprised by the response.

A queue formed outside the little store, quite filling the approach alleyway, of women delighted at the prospect of obtaining American nylons which were hard to come by even on the black market in Germany. Mr Tadd served the ladies as fast as he could take their money, although he considered the queue a trifle too big for quiet trading. What he did not know was that the queue extended beyond the alleyway out of his sight round the corner, going back half a mile past the Police Headquarters into the Kaiser Dam main thoroughfare.

At the Police Headquarters an officer came out to know why the entrance was blocked. A lady told him, "A consignment of nylon stockings has arrived from America, so naturally we are queuing up before they are all gone."

Being accustomed to rationing, shortages and queues the officer posted two of his men to keep the entrance clear into the

Police Headquarters, but took no other action than to phone his wife to tell her that she should hurry round because a big Berlin store near his office was selling American nylons. Meanwhile, Mr Tadd had cancelled his lunch rather than disappoint the women still waiting in the alley outside the store, some of whom were remarking that they now understood why there was a nation-wide shortage of stockings, and, judging by what they could see inside the store, in America too.

On the afternoon of that fateful day the police officer began to receive traffic reports warning of considerable pedestrian congestion by the Tiergarten and further back to the Brandenburg Gate. Also such a vast concourse of people had gathered in the Victory Column area that riot police might be required to disperse them. News of some political demonstration in the city centre filtered back to Mr Tadd, but, being a foreigner, he rightly ignored such rumours and continued selling nylons, irrespective of his customers' political persuasions.

It was the Russians who finally brought matters to a head, reporting to the Allied Commission that a great civilian army was massing along the border opposite them, and that many women from East Germany had attempted to cross the frontier to join it. But when the German authorities tried to track down the source of the uprising nobody knew what it was about. The estimated 50,000 people along the Tiergarten had no idea why they were there but they thought it was probably a rally. Moreover, the police cars could no longer get through the crowds to investigate.

The paradox of the situation was that Mr Tadd stopped selling nylons that night, not because of police interference but because the disturbances in the city centre were spreading into the British Sector and he did not want to become involved in non-profit politics. According to the story the police were three weeks getting on to Mr Tadd as the cause of the troubles, and his bitterest complaint was being caught red-handed for the simple reason he had not realized he was the cause in the first place.

As Dr Collins glared at the redundant classroom heater and heard about *Fancy Free the Second,* he sensed in his heart that not only must the story be true but also he divined who supplied the nylons to Mr Tadd in the beginning.

FOUR

I discovered the truth about Miss Dewar in a very strange way, but in an all too commonplace setting—the staff party. Staff parties, where the undrinkable may lead to the unthinkable—and sometimes does. Where elderly teachers one thought were passing peacefully away in their offices insist on singing unidentifiable ballads about aged mothers waiting for the return of lifeboats, and nice spinster ladies revealing themselves as bottomless pits for brandy-and-ginger.

Tonight's belle of the ball was unmistakably Rosalind Banger, and I have noticed how beautiful, glamorous girls often labour under the handicap of most unromantic names before marrying someone like O'Nion. Miss Banger taught Biology and she often taught it under the additional handicap of a hangover from Cudford night life the next morning, cutting up ox eyes in class wearing an expression far removed from biological dedication.

But tonight she looked radiant, and there was plenty of her to look radiant because she was barely keeping inside one of those cocktail dresses dolls wear at parties that show nine-tenths of the iceberg. In fact it couldn't fairly be described as a dress, being more accurately a clever device to prevent her sitting there in the nude. The men were chasing her like relay runners and I despised them for it.

I ignored her, standing by the settee aloof and immune to her charms, marvelling at the way these men who should know better were hanging on her every word. It was nauseating, especially Mr Whittle, who taught Art with a spray-gun. He was sitting next to Rosalind fawning over her as if she was part of the cold buffet, pretending to nibble the two red cherries suspended from her neck-band. I gave him a surreptitious shove with my hip, unnoticed in the crowd, whereupon he stood up unexpectedly to exclaim that he had swallowed an artificial cherry.

"Water," I advised, simultaneously occupying his seat for the next cherry.

"Do bring me another Vodka-and-whatsit, sweetheart," Rosalind called after him. "Hallo, next sweetheart—why if it isn't Peterkins! Had an accident on the way to the party?"

"Rugby. Somebody had to stop the Welsh. You see, I'm not one of your poofy boys."

"You can say that again!"

I laughed debonairly to let her see I could take a joke against myself. I did not worry about my looks any more because it actually helped with some dolls by bringing out the mother in them to protect me from further damage up front. I remember Belinda, who once cried as she kissed me as though I had been run over in the street, and Hilda Longbothem used to say that going out with me made her look beautiful. So a girl like Hilda needed me urgently.

"You're so big and craggy that it makes me feel all female, Peter. I regard you as a challenge."

"You certainly look all female," I smirked, trying not to look like a challenge who has just seen the statue of a Greek fertility goddess. By comparison with Rosalind, Hilda Longbothem resembled a little old man.

"May I feel your face, Peter?" she giggled.

"Not until we're married." I could have bitten my tongue off the moment the words were out, but it was my stock reply to women, in the days when I was available, who could no longer keep their hands off my clock. It had not been flattering to discover how women in love desired nothing so much as to embrace me passionately in order to fondle my face for the purpose of straightening it. Belinda used to stick a finger in the corner of my mouth and push it to the left before kissing me, while Hilda insisted on shoring up my nose with a clothes peg grip lest the pressure of courtship should make it worse. Olga loved to caress me with fingers spread wide all over my face like a stretch-frame until everything was grouped to her satisfaction, whispering, "Now kiss me quickly before I have to let go."

"Women don't bother me nowadays—I've overcome it," I told Rosalind airily, hoping the poor girl's heart would not break against my icy fortitude and reminding myself of Smollett's apt quotation, 'He was formed for the ruin of our sex'. Surely even Rosalind could see it was hopeless.

A disconcerting amount of Rosalind leaned over me for a two-point landing, so that momentarily I thought the staff had assembled around my bed. Tossing back her hair from my face I sat there with unruffled panache.

"Why don't you like girls any more, Peter?"

"They bore me nowadays. Life is too short for trifles."

"Then why are you trembling?"

"Am I? I hadn't noticed."

"You keep spilling your drink."

"Oh that? Just a passing nervous breakdown."

"You won't believe this, Peter, but I'm extremely fond of men."

"Shall I fetch you some more?"

"Don't tease. It's you I like because you're a new kind of experience for me."

"First time you ever had to make do with just one?"

Here it was again, I thought; women being attracted to me like children want to be scared by horror stories.

"I don't care what the others say, Peter, I don't think you're ugly one little bit. I think you're beautiful, like a rock fault on a mountain."

"Thank you, Rosalind. I'll try not to let it go to my head." If this was her idea of a compliment I might have to gently reprove her with a fist up her nostrils.

Our school was a strict one where Biology mistresses were not encouraged to flatten male staff on the settee, even under the heading of Social Activities, and people were beginning to stare. Slumped down defensively in the seat, I seemed to be surrounded by Rosalind's bare shoulders and bust exposed by low tide, and somewhat anaesthetized by perfume she purchased in a bottle shaped like a glass hunting-horn, labelled Mating Call. I realized I was not in conventional promotion pose if Dr Collins passed by, but Rosalind's sinuous lips began to explore my face in search of bone damage and scar parks. Worse still, I could diagnose rust attacking my iron will.

"You remind me of that lovely Crusader knight lying on his tomb in Cudford Cathedral, darling," Rosalind whispered when she reached the T-junction by my left ear.

"Don't try to buy me with flattery," I replied. The face of the statue in question had been hit by one of Cromwell's cannonballs right between the eyes, so I managed to contain my conceit.

"And just as dead," she added, endeavouring—like others before her—to reopen my disused nostril.

"Try a pair of pliers while you're at it." I jested thus solely to prevent my weakening to feminine wiles one tiny fraction by ripping her dress off in front of Dr Collins and his lady.

"Why are you so cold, Peter? Don't you want things to happen tonight?"

"Like being sacked on the spot?"

"I mean afterwards—when you come to my flat."

"I can't, Rosalind ... I've taken a vow."

"Taken a vow! What ever for?"

"I've vowed never again to . . . er. . . ."

"Yes, darling?"

"Never again to, well, kill wildlife. I've even given up fishing."

"What the hell has that got to do with us?"

"I thought you ought to know, that's all."

"I'm not suggesting we leave here at midnight to go fishing or organize a foxhunt."

"Well, that's a weight off my mind."

"Is that why you're trembling and sweating so?"

"I'm rusting badly."

"There's something you ought to know as well, Peter. I suffer from hay-fever in the spring."

"You drag unsuspecting farmers into barns, eh? Ha, ha, ha, ha! But what does that matter tonight with no harvest moon, darling?"

"About as much as your vow, honey. Now try to square up your lips and kiss me where it counts."

Lying inert at my feet, locked with rigor mortis, was my conscience. I began to pant, as men do who are being forced into love against their will and know they are on to a good thing, and Rosalind was the softest creature I had held in my arms since my childhood balloons.

A voice in my other ear said, "That sort of conduct in the staff room won't make you Head of Department—even in Liberal Studies." It was Mr Mould.

"But it'll make me a lot happier," I gasped.

"Happiness is £-shaped, Peter. Put her down and meet misery."

Suddenly I found myself being introduced to a stranger, but I was unable to stand up so I shook hands like an invalid. Mr Mould was saying, "This is Mr White, Biology Adviser to Cudford Education Committee."

"Why?" I asked stupidly.

"My oath, what a man!" Rosalind was saying. "He looks like a Greek god on wheels. To think I come under him!"

"Delighted to meet you Miss Banger," the Greek god purred in a voice like a distant buzz-saw in the forest. "I am sure we shall be very happy working together."

Rosalind was happy right now, holding on to the man's hand long after the shake. He reminded me of Rex Fairbrother in the women's magazine stories, but up to now I thought he only existed in the colour illustrations, leaning on a farm gate to ask unsophisticated Madge the way to Magna Manor and deeply bronzed by the Chelsea sun.

"Are you stopping?" I inquired, to break the seance.

"Only about three weeks. Mustn't leave the kids too long."

"Oh, so you're married?"

"Widower, I'm afraid. Air crash, you understand?"

"Oh—I'm sorry." Sorry he hadn't been in the plane too. The only thing spared me so far was that he was rich.

"I expect you're wealthy," I blurted out.

"Well, my wife left a considerable amount of money."

"Naturally."

"And the insurance compensation was exceedingly generous."

"Of course."

"Oh, the poor children," Rosalind sighed. "I adore children."

I stared at her in amazement. Rosalind, who swore every day at four o'clock that she never wanted to see another brat as long as she lived, and that when she married it would be sterilization all round.

"Please fetch Rex a drink, there's a pet, Peter," Rosalind said without looking at me. I bade farewell to my seat and went to the improvised bar for a double cyanide with ice. I returned feeling like the Hunchback of Notre Dame with 'flu, only to discover a wall of men round the settee where there was an excellent aerial view of Rosalind's coastline.

"Have you seen this fellow's Aston Martin in the car park?" Mr Whittle asked me with unnatural zest for Aston Martins.

I ignored it. "Pass this drink through to Apollo and shut up, Whittle. Tell him Quasimodo brought it from the belfry."

"He sure is a nifty dresser, Pook; looks like a model straight out of *Town* magazine."

"I'm not one of your poofy peacocks. I wear the rags of yesteryear so folks will accept me for what I am, not what I've got on my back."

"So you don't mind loneliness?"

"You will be surprised to know that I belong to *Retreat* in order to give up women completely."

"That's like joining a youth club to prevent you growing younger."

"Watch how I smile bravely through my tears, Whittle, and don't pester me to paint my portrait."

"The Head won't allow my work to be hung in the Gents."

"He prefers the old-fashioned toilet-rolls?"

Relations between Mr Whittle and me had been strained ever since I defined modern art as 'You throw it—I'll spread it.' and Mr Mould had mounted his boots on a plinth in the entrance hall over the caption: *Agony*. We had been protesting against Mr Whittle decorating the school with his modern works of art ranging from twenty coat-hangers entitled *Absent Friends,* to an entirely red canvas hanging in the staff room called *Red Indian*. Next to it Mr Mould had hung a sheet of white card labelled *Absent Red Indian*.

But our chief grievance was the statue in the playground of surplus drain-pipes Mr Whittle christened *Ethos of Education*. However, this problem had been settled in an unexpected manner because when the Corporation dustmen came in during the holidays to clear up they carted it away. When charged by Mr Whittle of instigating this crime against culture, Mr Mould declared that dustmen were experts at recognizing rubbish without assistance from him.

It was then that Mr Whittle went to work with zest to decorate the great wall of the Assembly Hall, reminding us of Michelangelo in the Sistine chapel, except that Mr Whittle used squeegees and spray-gun instead of brushes. As the mighty canvas neared completion bets were laid in the staff room as to what it was. Mr Pearson put his money on *Explosion in Jam Factory,* while Mr Hamble favoured *Sunrise over Scottish Kipper*. Mr Franklin suggested *Warts without Cromwell,* but

Mr Figgin saw it as a war scene depicting the bombing of the Egg Marketing Board.

Mr Mould, however, pointed out that the subject had to be of religious significance, and was in fact *Jonah and the Whale*. He later amended the title to *Jonah in the Whale* on the grounds that Mr Whittle had created a life-size reproduction of a whale's stomach in section. The mystery was deepened by a board at ground level which said 'Wet Paint', as though this was the title—and by the fact that next day the board had been sabotaged to read 'Wet Painter'.

The problem was finally solved at Assembly, when Mr Whittle announced to the world—and although he was addressing the world he had narrowed his gaze down to Mr Mould—that the massive work of art represented *Judas the Betrayer* against a background of John the Baptist's head on a silver salver.

By bending down I was able to present my bodiless hand holding the drink to Mr White but there was no way through for the rest of me. I stood at the rear of the crowd like a latecomer to a road accident, despising these weak-kneed men for their sycophancy over a ripe tomato and cursing my luck, when I caught a Scottish ballad in the air which I recognized as Karen talking to me in the tartan dialect.

"Air ye a wee bit sare, Peter?" she inquired, apparently in code.

I laughed deprecatingly. "Men! Thank goodness I'm not like this lot. I've seen more strength of character down a mouse hole."

"She's awfa' bonnie, Peter."

"Not half so awfa' bonnie as that slick body-snatcher."

"He's awfa' charming, Peter."

"That's his bedside manner. He wouldn't look so charming with a fat-eye half way up."

"I do believe you've fallen for Rosalind."

I laughed incredulously—which isn't easy. "Rosalind! I was

merely playing hard to get, testing my will-power to ensure my won't-power is stronger—like they test-drive a car to near destruction."

"Then why were you kissing each other?"

"She was cracking up, so I played along with it. I hadn't the heart to stop her. Then the British Museum sent Apollo round to save her from herself."

"I don't know how you can be so strong, Peter."

"Nothing really, Karen. Clean living and hard work are the basics of course, but the *Retreat System* builds up your iron will, together with the tablets. When you reach my stage, women are just small men in kilts."

"Why do you drive yourself so hard, Peter?"

"Because I want to be a celebrated author, so I mustn't dissipate my energies on women." One of the great mysteries of life to me just now was how I was not becoming a celebrated author and had been fined six times by *Retreat,* incidentally establishing a record for the course. Instinct was now warning me that if I did not get rid of this Scottish lassie fast it would be £7 and a new record. The pages of our magazine were full of letters from grateful readers who had given it up for good and were now rugby internationals or captains of industry, yet our President hinted to me in his last written reprimand that the only thing keeping me on roll was his money-back guarantee to a new life free from the lusts of the flesh—which in my case, he implied, might be in the next world. Worse still, his Physiognomy Department had studied my photograph and was baffled as to why I should be bothered by women at all.

Karen gave a little smile. "Perhaps I can help you, Peter."

"I can't force you to leave Cudford."

"No, I mean help you here."

"Help me here!" When you're treed in the jungle by a lion you don't count on him fetching you a ladder to get down.

"I could type the stories for you."

69

"But I have to write them in English—I'm sorry, Karen, that slipped out unconsciously." Help me by typing the stories! *McPook in Porridge-land*—a passionate regional novel now reduced to ninepence at your local su⌣ermarkets, or free with Jumbo Oats.

I gave Karen the old heart-breaker smile to let her see she was wasting her time. "Just for the record, honey, you are an extremely attractive doll, but you can see what you're up against. Don't cry for me, baby—find someone else."

"But I don't think you're ugly, Peter, honestly."

"Maybe you need glasses." I said this merely to cover her naive misinterpretation of a dramatic situation and save her embarrassment. What she really needed was a crash course on tact and how to use it. Above the general chatter we could distinctly hear Rosalind telling Rex how he oozed charm like a rubber tree and that just to look at him made her feel pregnant, so I waited for Karen to say that just to look at me made her feel ill. But she was regarding me kindly, like a diver who has finally located the wreck.

"Would you care for some lobster, sir?" a voice was asking. It was Crowhurst of the buck teeth and fringe, who had volunteered to hand round the refreshments. Crowhurst had a knack of volunteering for jobs which did not exist until he volunteered.

"Lobster, eh? My favourite."

Crowhurst handed me a shrimp on a finger of toast.

"Would you care for some salmon, miss?" he persisted.

Karen received a sardine on toast.

"Sir, could you explain to me how the Carnot Cycle works?"

"What, at a party, Crowhurst? Besides, I haven't had a bike since the old Hercules three-speed job."

"I think he means something about reversible heat engines," Karen whispered to me.

"That's Mr Figgin's department, Crowhurst, so buzz off and

play with the electric meat-slicer. He had me on the Doppler Effect on Concords yesterday, Karen. Mr Mould says he must be transferred to Grammar School immediately or put down."

"Put down to 4B?"

"No, dear, done in."

Although Mr Mould had declared that since Pastoral Care was the order of the day we were all State shepherds, I often oozed love and affection over the children that was not always sincere, akin to making a fuss of a cobra particularly in the case of a deprived child named Rosemary, who bore a striking resemblance to Sir Winston Churchill with curls and smelt strongly of wet carpet. Rosemary, who saw me as Dad, was handicapped by a cleft palate which required her to call me Hir. I feared the class might laugh at her but they not only took her chatter for granted but understood her, which was more than I could.

This class was mine once a week for speech therapy, so we read little plays in which Rosemary always demanded the main role. Each lesson commenced the same way, by Rosemary crying out, "Honk honk honk honk honk, hir."

"What did she say?" I asked my interpreter, one Fred.

"She wants to be Joan of Arc, sir," Fred replied, appalled by my obtuseness.

"Good, Rosemary shall be Joan of Arc."

"Honk, honk, hir," Rosemary thanked me. Quickly I scanned the pages to see the long speeches demanded of our heroine, wondering if I could stand it without ear-plugs, and praying she would not ask me to pronounce a word half-way down. Whatever I said—like Ogre; "Say O-ger, Rosemary."—she always repeated it as Honk-honk, so it did not seem vitally important. Every Thursday after we had honked our way through forty minutes of inconceivably boring play-reading the children loved to perform without pauses or intonation or expression, I reeled into the staff room like one who has been

71

imperfectly coshed by night.

I was often joined in the horizontal position by an exhausted teacher called Mr. Long, an ex-college lecturer who had joined us because under the new system he could earn more money in school. His methods were extremely formal and old-fashioned, which was surprising because as a lecturer he had preached non-streaming, non-setting and Look-at-the-Lovely-Clouds method, designed to make everybody equal even if they could not read or write.

Mr Mould used to say to Mr Long, "Sports Day should be abolished, Long, because then we can no longer conceal from the public that some children can run faster than others."

Mr Long was a strong supporter of Free Discipline, but at our school he put it into practice by bashing the kids, roaring non-academic oaths and physically jamming their heads into text-books, informing his Maker and the entire teaching block that he would be forced to murder the next pupil who spoke, though he lose his pension rights in the process.

Mr Long's book on modern education, *Don't Hold Them Back,* came under constant scrutiny by Mr Mould, who, when Mr Long clouted Fred Rubble, inquired if the *Them* in the title referred to the staff rather than the children. Mr Mould also wanted to know why Mr Long wrote of 'Exuberant youth in search of Truth', when today he was calling them vicious little yobs. Mr Long admitted that it was one thing to write about education from an ivory tower but quite another to enter the front line and do the job, and as a result his views had been slightly modified. However, he insisted that his theories were basically sound if only he could control the pupils long enough to explain them.

"What he means, Peter," Mr Mould remarked to me, "is that if he could have the children chained up and gagged he would be able to introduce his Free Discipline to them. At the moment he's introduced the Reign of Terror instead."

Although in a reputedly tough area, Cudford School was remarkably free of the troubles so dear to the popular media. There was no drug problem, and our sole case of serious violence in a whole year was that of three girls beating up another and knocking out a tooth. I found the children friendly, fun-loving, quite keen to learn and fond of their school. Crowhurst apart, they were not particularly bright academically, though our examination results were excellent and the school produced at least six teachers from its ranks. The range of pupils was wide, from often unstable remedials to outstanding young adults with impeccable records.

Crowhurst exposed his ivories at me in what he imagined was an engaging smile over the shrimp joke, so I returned the traditional teacher-pupil rapport smile by baring my teeth only. Thus encouraged, Crowhurst smirked archly at Miss Dewar to indicate Romance, phase one, as though he regarded himself as a pasty-faced Cupid bearing ambrosia-on-toast, and enlarged his eyes suggestively at her bust-line.

"Lucky old sir!" he chuckled.

I grinned affectionately at him, wondering what his parents would say if he had to be assisted home with his front teeth straightened.

"You worry too much about your looks, Peter," Karen advised me. "Girls should be pretty, not men. I don't like handsome men—they're so conceited and selfish. You're nice because you're, well, sort of rugged."

"Are you trying to tell me something, Karen?" I said this because girls always impressed on me how they did not fancy the pretty boys, and I always ended up dancing with Mrs Collins. One could only conclude that although girls did not like handsome men, they preferred them to me. Likewise during the Ladies' Choice Waltz I always stood up front in expectant pose, only to see girls dancing together under my very nose, until it puzzled me why nobody had invented a dance one could do on one's own. My ex-friend Honners once suggested I go on the floor alone during a quick-step, and tap-dance my way through the throng as if it was the done thing—an idea he mooted one night at the Cudford Palais in answer to my desperate plea that we dance with each other in the Goodnight Waltz. He added that although he would have to take me home as usual he wasn't going to dance for the privilege. Even in unromantic mass dances like the Hokey-Cokey and Knees Up Mother Brown I had to fight tooth and nail to keep in, while in barn dances I often discovered that the next space I was meant to occupy was already full up. Once during a Progression Waltz the MC ordered me off the floor for trying to join the next couple and dance as a threesome, and immediately the Dashing White Sergeant began I found myself the only sergeant with no pair of girls waiting for him on the next move. Likewise in the Paul Jones, every time the music stopped I froze opposite a blank space, so had to leave the floor even when I tried to cheat. Another thing I learned when asking ladies to dance was that many of them attended these functions with a broken leg which required them to sit out until a special man arrived who was trained to dance with the injured. I phoned Cudford General Hospital to inquire if I might enrol for such a course in order to dance with their casualties, but the Matron grew quite angry and slammed the phone down.

"What I'm trying to tell you, Peter, is that in your own inimitable way you're quite sexy," Karen smiled.

"I know, dear. I attract women like a talking toad. You can't get more inimitable than that."

"What holds you back is that you're not sure of yourself."

"Unfortunately, Karen, it's being so sure of myself that holds me back." This girl would tell a fat man who couldn't see over his stomach that he was underweight.

"I like you anyway, Peter," she said coyly.

"You should have joined the Salvation Army, dear. They

need your type."

"So I'm determined to take you in hand and show you what you've been missing in the world."

"That's because most girls would only go out with me when it was dark. Would you come out with me in the daylight?"

"Oh, Peter, don't be so ridiculously macabre. Of course I'll go out with you in daylight."

"I mean in public—not across the moors."

"I shall get extremely cross if you persist in pretending you're some kind of monster. Just to let you see how silly it is I'm going to kiss you right here in front of everyone."

"Promise you're not just trying to kiss it better."

"Oh shut up and come here, you daft wee bairn!"

Once again the staff turned their heads in puzzled curiosity as Karen took me in her arms and kissed my defenceless lips long and passionately, wondering how it was that, against all the odds, I invariably ended up on target pinned down by the female embrace in abject surrender. Personally, I considered my secret came under the general heading of Darwin's theory of natural selection.

I had even forgotten about the £7 fine.

FIVE

My teaching career was not helped by the next game against the London Irish wherein I was carried off at the critical moment when we were holding them at 88 points to 3, under the impression that I had performed the remarkable feat of swallowing the ball whole. I indicated by mime where the ball lay in my gullet, rather than hold up the game, but our trainer bent over my body to assure me they were now using the reserve ball, so not to worry. Instead, he peered up my nostrils as if in search of the London Irish scrum half's boot.

The upshot of this disastrous match was that I spoke with the voice of a patient suffering from giant adenoids as big as cauliflowers. I had only to speak on a bus or in a shop for everyone to turn and stare at the man with the Donald Duck voice. Mr Mould said I reminded him of an early phonograph recording of Queen Victoria being transmitted over the first wireless, when she was apparently addressing the nation from the bottom of a mine-shaft. Mr Franklin produced the original celluloid record of *God Bless the Prince of Wales,* sung by a tenor who seemingly wore a clothes-peg on his nose, and played it on his HMV horn gramophone for my benefit.

Consequently I resorted to handing little notes to shop assistants, rather than alarm them with my new noise which made customers think there was an ambulance going by. Old Dr Mernst advised me the impediment was only temporary and would probably clear up before he died, and Dr Collins suggested I base my lessons mainly on blackboard work in the classroom.

For obvious reasons I was taken off interviewing irate parents in the nut house, as we referred to the interview room. This public relations chore was done chiefly by the Deputy Head, Mr Hamble, who employed what he called the Hamble Strategy for this purpose. The technique was for the Secretary to usher the angry parent into the nut house to cool off as long as possible, on the precept that it is difficult to maintain maximum fury for half-an-hour if you are alone, any more than a pole vaulter can remain for any length of time at the apex of his jump.

The next step was to send in a defuser in the person of Mrs Willoughby, on whom the angry parent could vent his or her rage until they discovered that Mrs Willoughby was only an office cleaner who had come in to dust, and was partially deaf. This took the steam right out of most parents because even normal conversation with Mrs Willoughby was exhausting in the extreme, mainly because she never looked at you but just talked you into the ground, dragging you into the bottomless pit of what had become known locally as the Willoughby Financial Collapse. Some parents left the nut house to seek refuge in the corridor, while others sat back dazed and bemused under the barrage of the Willoughby saga, delivered on the television principle that the actor continues talking even if your house is on fire.

This was Mr Hamble's cue to enter bearing coffee and biscuits, and to hold a card up to Mrs Willoughby's thick spectacles which read 'That will be all for now, thank you, Mrs Willoughby'.

Like most people who are over-vociferous about their rights, angry parents often forgot that others have rights too, as Mr Hamble reminded them by handing out a copy of the school rules and an invitation to join our Parent-Teacher Association the moment they opened their mouths. Their grievances were so often based on the strongly biased and emotive tales of their offspring, who were themselves trying to pass the buck for their own misdemeanours.

A common complaint was theft by other children of coats or equipment. Petty theft bedevilled Cudford School, from cash to jewellery, but the problem of looking after a thousand coats was huge. Fortunately, Mr Hamble was often able to trace a missing coat by walking the parent and child throughout the buildings until the child remembered where he had misplaced it—perhaps in a desk or on the playing-field—whereupon it was not unknown for him to have to defend the child from the parent.

Our community consisted in the main of pupils who were pleasingly honest, but we were plagued by a minority who could not keep their fingers off anything even if they did not want it. Nothing was safe, from toilet rolls and electric bulbs to file paper and drawing-pins.

Just as Mr Crowhurst did not want his son to learn anything not directly connected with his future career, such as Games, PE, Art or Religious Knowledge, so Mr Rubble did not want his son to learn anything not connected with passing the entrance examination to his own employers, Cudford Abattoirs Ltd; an examination so low down on the list that even finding the premises to take it counted as a promising sign. Mr Rubble, who suffered severely from the physical rigours of alcohol and the mental stress of Bingo reminded me of a statue erected to commemorate a defeat. He had never fully recovered from his son's failure in the above examination, which he took as a personal humiliation imposed upon him by the school.

"I have come to take Fred home," he informed Mr Hamble, "because I don't hold with my son being kept back in late detention."

Fred was being detained for being late to school as was his wont—late, that is, inasmuch as he had overslept and arrived just in time for dinner, which he had free.

"I'm sorry, Mr Rubble, but Fred was late so he must obey the rules and stay behind the extra half hour. It's not a very severe punishment really—some of the children ask if they may be kept in anyway because they prefer it to going home. For example, the boy you will observe reading a book in the corner does that every afternoon because—believe it or not in this day and age—he is not allowed to read at home. His father claims

78

that turning the pages disturbs his television watching, and the lad is not permitted to read in his bedroom because it is a waste of electric light."

"Well, I want Fred to have homework so he can sit that exam again. Don't you teach my son nothing in this place?"

"We have done our best, Mr Rubble, but Fred does not wish to be taught—as we indicated every six months on his reports, but we heard nothing from you until he failed the test in his fourth year."

"I still want him to have homework, understand?"

"We had to stop Fred's homework in the past on three counts. One, he did not do it; two, we could not get our books back; three, a boy who does not do school work is most unlikely to do homework."

"Well, I'm taking Fred home right now. It's against the law to keep him after school—I know my rights." Mr Rubble held up his right fist, so Mr Hamble backed off. He did not consider that Pastoral Care included sparring with parents.

"School ends officially at four o'clock, Mr Rubble, though most children are released at three-thirty. Those who are receiving extra tuition or are being kept in, leave at the official end of the school day, four o'clock."

"Don't try to pull the wool over my eyes by a technicality, mate. My son goes home when the rest do. I want him out of here right now."

Mr Hamble smiled his special teacher-parent smile. "Certainly, Mr Rubble, there goes the four o'clock bell so Fred is all yours. Good-day to you, sir."

But the majority of parents were extremely cooperative and genuinely interested in their children's progress, as evinced by the way they supported our Open Nights, though we seldom saw those parents we most wanted to make contact with. Like us, the parents were also worried by the local gang warfare which played such a part in the children's lives outside school.

Whatever names they went under—Mods versus Rockers, Skinheads versus Greasers—it seemed most pupils had to join one side or the other, with all the petty, and often vicious, code of gang activity. Their main preoccupation seemed to be finding excuses for fights, chiefly over their girl-friends, but fights based on the idea that the safest bet was for a number of one side to set upon one individual of the other side, knock him down, then get the boot in. Sometimes girls would deal with one of their own number in like fashion.

Bravery was not high on their list of membership requirements, because they preferred to run away if the odds were not heavily in their favour. They figured eight to one was about right. Some of their nastier little rats played it really safe and beat up girls instead, like Stephen Link who waylaid a girl by night, punched her around—then ran away just in case.

These formed part of the minority who were now compelled to stay at school till sixteen, and to all the educational experts, lecturers, do-gooders and politicians our cry was this—stop talking about it, stop writing about it and come into school to do the job yourselves.

We suffered severely at the hands of the educational experts with their new ideas, systems and theories they imposed us, always taking good care not to be involved themselves on the ground floor. We had a maxim in the staff room that to get on in this profession one had to be a crackpot. The secret seemed to be based on the antonym principle—take any accepted, well-tried educational procedure, scrap it and introduce its opposite.

Over the years with the ever-changing fashion in education we witnessed every whim and theory they could dream up for us. No more text-books; abolish classroom walls so everybody can work in one enormous hall; eliminate the time-table; team teaching; no streaming; teachers must not teach, only advise; desks are redundant, all children can sit together; manual work should replace written work; don't learn anything by heart;

abolish examinations; spelling is old hat; grammar is dead; work on the parents, not the children; educate the pupils socially, not academically; abolish school uniform, the house system and prefects; abolish the form teacher; abolish the subject teacher; abolish the Headmaster; abolish school governors; divide the week into blocks of time; split the day into minutes of time; organize the school into modules; obtain complete flexibility by abolishing classes; pastoral care above all else; visit every pupil's home on a rota basis; television teaching is the answer; closed-circuit television is the answer; teaching-machines is the answer; appoint pupil advisers; implement tutor bases; all lessons must revolve around a theme; all lessons must be integrated within the curriculum; all lessons must be based on the school's immediate environment; Liberal Studies is the answer; scrap all subject divisions; School is Fun. . . .

The list is endless, depending on the current fashion, the school's locality and the eccentricities—not forgetting the ambitions—of one's Headmaster or Headmistress. Some of the ideas were good but the teaching profession on the whole seems incapable of moderation, too often jumping from one untried bandwagon to the next without a stepping-stone half-way, usually without consideration for pupils, parents or rank-and-file staff. Somce Heads, too, are terrified of being thought old-fashioned or trailing in the wake of the progressives—sometimes with disastrous results.

How often did pupils tell me, "I enjoyed school till they started the new system. They've given us so much freedom that there's nothing worthwhile left. I think they're trying to drive everybody crazy—the teachers as well as us. All I want to do now is leave."

How often did parents tell me, "I'm worried about my child's career, but that's the last thing the school seems to think about lately."

How often did teachers themselves tell me, "This school has

changed from a child-centred world to a system-centred world—and I'm looking for another post."

Another disillusioned teacher told me, "Unfortunately, educational gimmickry is the short-cut to promotion and we are the victims. It is like telling footballers they will have a much better game if they are freed from the old-fashioned restrictions of rules and referees, even if that means the sport itself disappears in the process."

We suffered from some educational gimmickry at Cudford when we listened to four hours of gibberish masquerading under the name of Shakespeare in order that the producer might become Drama Adviser to the County of Cudford. Or the time when I woke up to discover I was no longer a teacher but a Module Coordinator. I knew enough of the jargon to realize a Coordinator was the current euphemism for someone in charge of others, replacing such terms as schoolmaster or Head which smacked too strongly of master and servant. If a naval Captain were in teaching his designation might well be Crew Coordinator or Fleet Adviser—even a Gunnery Officer would become Armaments Counsellor or Noise Abatement Monitor. A Petty Officer would cause much heart-searching, finally emerging as an Intermediate Hortative Mentor.

"What is a Module, Mr Mould?" I inquired.

"Something to do with space exploration, Peter. The Americans use them in their moon shots, such as the service module and the lunar module."

"That's going to be awkward because I'm one right here in school. I'm a Module Coordinator."

"You should worry—I'm a Horizontal Subject Correlator."

"Who is trying to flee the classroom by promotion now?"

"Probably Whittle. He's been in conference with the Head a lot lately, explaining his scheme to let the pupils choose their own subjects and go to the teachers they prefer if they want advice whenever they feel like it. Whittle knows the Head dreads the annual chore of constructing the new timetable, so he's dreamed up a way to abolish it altogether. On the other hand, those pupils who like a time-table can make up their own and give it to the Head."

"But where do we fit in?"

"We go to our classrooms—sorry, research space areas— and wait there to see if anybody turns up for advice. This is what Whittle calls Flexible Modulation. Collins and Hamble struggle with the new time-table every year for about a month, but these days it's become so complex—what with streaming, setting, blocking, options, Group Work and Team Teaching—that towards the end of the operation they're like two gamblers throwing dice. Even the County's computer fell down on the job. Whittle saw this problem and produced his new Flexible Modulation. Then he told the Head about it, but the smart boy waited till near the end until he threw in an aside that his system incidentally abolished the time-table. What he didn't disclose was that it also abolishes the Head. So Whittle worked the Head in as CM—Centripetal Moderator—and Hamble will be known as SC— Surrogate Consultant."

"What do they do then?"

"My guess is that their main function will be to pacify angry parents and explain to them about progressive education. They will also issue a daily bulletin to the staff to let them know where they are, what is happening to them, and where they think the children will be."

"Won't it all be rather confusing, Mr Mould?"

Mr Mould puffed his pipe. "You miss the whole point of the scheme, Peter. The paramount aim is Whittle's promotion, either to a traditional school as Head or to a College of Education as Lecturer—anywhere out of the classroom. No one in his right mind would stay in a situation like this one. The secondary aim is to eliminate the time-table for Collins. Thirdly, Collins can meet other Heads and boast that he is avant garde in sweeping away the shackles of the past, then put the pressure on by asking why they aren't avant garde, too.

"It sounds terrible, Mr Mould."

"Now be fair to Whittle, Peter. Only man bites dog is news, remember? No good inventing a car with wheels — you have to invent a car without wheels for instant success. Believe me, Peter, if Whittle were commissioned to invent a lifeboat which wouldn't capsize he'd design one that was already upside-down. Mind you, he's done an extremely thorough job— even the caretaker emerges as EW, or Enviromnental Warden."

"How does Whittle himself fit into the scheme?"

Mr Mould re-lit the burned-down bowl of his pipe and smiled through the smog. "Ah, where indeed? You see, Peter, a scheme of this magnitude must have a gaffer, a trouble-shooter, to iron out the bumps and knock it into shape. So Whittle does not fit into the plan—he fits outside of it as CE, or Cybernetics Evaluator. Note how the word comes from the Greek, meaning a helmsman who steers the ship while we row ourselves into the sea-bed. Thus our friend Whittle is able to desert the classroom immediately, rather than having to await promotion to the peaceful cloisters of our academic retreats."

"He's really sharp, Mr Mould."

"Even sharper. The scheme is so complex in its machinations to simplify schooling—Whittle sees us like a huge power station operated by one man seated at a console—that Dr Collins is understandably prevented from seeing he is no longer Head, but a supernumerary under Whittle, which some people might argue is to the good. Whittle confided in me that he had great difficulty in modifying the scheme to include Collins at all, let alone as a figurehead, and had even considered the possibility of asking him to retire on full pay or golden handshake, rather than suffer sitting alone and workless in an office as Centripetal Moderator as though he had been sent to Coventry."

"How ever did he get round that one then, Mr Mould?"

"He has arranged for traditional-type work files that Collins can understand to be sent into his office daily to stop him going potty and to give the impression he is still Head. These, naturally, are dummy files which cannot damage the new system, and his phone is so linked that Whittle always answers at the other end, no matter what number he dials."

"When do you think the scheme will be fully operational, Mr Mould?"

"Whittle has run into two strokes of bad luck, Peter. The first is ROSLA—raising of the school leaving age to sixteen, a desperate expedient induced by politicians to relieve the strain on our jails and social security. The second is Comprehensive Education, better known as Compulsory Chaos, invented to abolish Grammar Schools and based on the theory that the good apples in a barrel will turn a bad apple good. Kindly note, Peter, how educational reform nowadays is modelled on the naval convoy, wherein the speed of the convoy is that of the slowest ship. Mr Whittle, who believes in equal opportunity for all except the bright pupils, has probably consulted his masters in Peking on the point, with the result that he is confident that once ROSLA and ComprehensiveEducation have been established here at Cudford the confusion will be so great that his Flexible Modulation policy will be the only way of keeping the school open."

"What do you think of it yourself, Mr Mould?"

"Die-hard that I am, Peter, I am by nature always suspicious of progress that marches boldly backwards. At least Dr Collins' present regime possesses the virtue of lurching fearlessly sideways against modern pressures to produce an illiterate, lazy, dissatisfied and purposeless society, well equipped to engineer its own downfall without further aid from our enemies abroad. Ye shall know them by their works, Peter—when I perceive my liberators and witness their deeds I flee terror-stricken back to the arms of my oppressors. "

I returned to the classroom feeling we were the last feeble outpost of the free world. The door was politely opened for me by Master Bill Gripping, underprivileged son of a wealthy dock crane-driver who, according to Bill, contrived with his wife to earn £130 a week. Bill had asked me to alter his name in my register to Bill Gripping instead of William Gripping because William smacked of class snobbery, and was in fact poofy—I had learned that many things were poofy, such as the Choir and non-pop music, while other things like poetry and shirt ties were crap. I discovered that everything Bill did not approve of were either poofy or crap, which did not leave much in life for the rest of us. Even Cudford United football team was crap, because Bill supported far-off Liverpool whom he had never seen.

Bill's outlook on life made my English Discussion lessons hard going, wherein he was able to answer local and world problems by one word. In desperation, I quoted the current pop protest songs—Why don't you listen to us?; just you keep quiet and hear us for a change; We gonna make you listen—and explained how I was listening like a big-eared bat on cave guard, only to learn that these songs were poofy because they were not sung by Bill's approved group. It seemed Bill's approved group was Rat Whiskers, who specialized in Yuk, which rather left me out on a limb. Yuk, I discovered, had no words and was strictly for listening to, not talking about, and anything outside of Yuk was crap—which, I sensed, included me.

The rest of the class listened boredly, longing to get on with the repetition exercise they loved so well. One of the many Linda's put her hand up.

"Yes, Linda? You wanted to add to our discussion of Yuk?"

"Can we get on with our work, sir?"

"What work is that, Linda?"

"Our vocabulary exercises, sir."

"Very well, Linda."

I shrank back baffled and discouraged. This meant sitting in a morgue for forty minutes, passive and unwanted, while the class dealt with their cursed words, making me feel about as welcome as a yodeller at a funeral. To pass the time whilst redundant I read through their book summaries. The class had been asked to read any book of their choice, then to summarize it as a prelude to tackling such works as *Jane Eyre, Animal Farm* and other examination favourites.

Stephen Webb had selected *The World Turned Red,* not, as I had thought, a study of Communism, but a gory description of the next war, which was to be won by the sword. There was a great deal of knacker's yard atmosphere in this book, as heads were lopped by single blows, followed by fountains of blood gushing up to repaint the ceilings. For a work on global war I thought the author had narrowed his theme by recording in precise detail the many parts of the body which might be severed by the sword, reminding me of an apprentice butcher's instruction chart.

Bill Gripping had chosen a paperback earthily titled *Get Stuffed,* illustrated by a gloomy cover of a nude girl wearing only a chef's hat as she prepared a turkey for the oven. But this was no cook book, being chiefly concerned with a Skinhead who prepared girls for bed, followed by What the Butler Saw sequences, plus mixed wrestling like a mattress manufacturer's durability test.

Of course, these paperbacks they garnered at our newsagents were tame stuff compared with the films our pupils saw every Saturday at the local cinema, where sex, sadism and violence were so commonplace that they laughed at them and cheered the actors on, even when the disintegration of bodies was shot in slow-motion for more detailed examination.

Even so, Linda's paper took me by surprise—not the content, but that she had written it. Linda was a pretty girl of fifteen, smartly dressed in the current fashion, quiet and conscientious in all she did. I knew that last week she had seen a film in which a soldier cut off a woman's breast in technicolor because she told me during our discussion on Art, yet I was unprepared for her summary. I knew also that when she and Bill Gripping had broken friends, as they called it, Bill had turned arsonist by scattering paper in the boys' toilet and setting fire to it. We averaged about one fire a year, usually in the toilets, either over a love affair or a teacher-pupil clash, plus bomb scares by phone from disgruntled pupils which meant evacuating the premises for an hour during the police search.

Linda wrote of a girl like herself who had been put up for auction by the local gang in order to go to the highest bidder, but oddly enough there were soon only two people left in the bidding—the gang leader and a girl. When this girl won Roz in the end I thought she intended to save her, not take Roz back to her flat and compel her to whip her with an iron chain. I told myself this was hardly *Little Women* stuff, but when the girl forced Roz to go out in the streets to murder men she did not even know and tore up her dress so she could wear the 'in' leather gear with boots I decided to skip to the last paragraph.

This was the unkindest cut of all. Linda had written, 'This is one of the best books I have ever read. In fact it was so exciting that I could not put it down, and I read it in a single day.'

I glanced across at Linda, absorbed in looking up these cursed words like *Abhor* and *Penultimate*, holding back her long shiny hair with the left hand so she could see to write. She appeared so virginal and sweet that it seemed impossible she was being reared on the modern diet of permissive books, films and television. How came this paradox that she—like most of the other girls—was so proper, almost prim, in her outlook?

One of my tasks was to take these girls and boys of the Fourth Year for sex instruction under the guise of Birth, Marriage and Old Age, primarily to relieve Mr Whittle that he might give more time to his scheme of Flexible Modulation, and—perhaps most vital of all in any new project—to plant the seed in Dr Collins' receptive mind that it was his own brain child really, and that Whittle was merely an admiring tool for its fruition. After his initial approach to the Head, Mr Whittle always referred to the scheme as "Your inspired idea, sir," or at worst, "My methodical collectanea of your own enlightened tenets over the years, sir," or even, "A presumptuous attempt on my part, sir, to bypass your characteristic modesty in these matters by revealing your educational prowess to the world."

To reinforce this impression the typed folder of the scheme was boldly headed 'Collins-Whittle Flexible Modulation Cartulary', yet when Mr Mould accidentally turned out Mr Whittle's locker in the staff room by night he discovered that the copies of the folder destined for the world were headed 'Whittle Flexible Modulation Cartulary'.

My eyes widened when they saw the diagrams in the set book on Birth. No birds-and-bees preliminaries here, but neat gynaecology for midwives from conception to delivery, with lots of labels and arrows. Nor was the male partner forgotten. He stood there from the waist down, x-rayed to show right through those parts not normally spoken about, as though the poor fellow was the victim of an enormous bacon-slicer.

"Clear, isn't it, sir?" Crowhurst grinned at me. Only he showed any sign of emotion; the rest, boys and girls seated as separately as they could manage, copied the diagrams into their folders as though we were reproducing a map of Italy.

"What is clear, Crowhurst?"

"How we do it, sir. Piston-and-sleeve job, like a motorbike. I wouldn't mind being an obstetrician when I leave school, sir. What do you think of sex before marriage, sir?"

"Delightful." The word jumped out before I could stop it, causing the girls to look up from their pelvises and Crowhurst to laugh shrilly.

"Naughty sir!" he beamed archly.

"I was joking, of course, class." It was too late.

"Do you agree with sex, sir?" Trap number two from Crowhurst, inviting the reply, "Sex agrees with me."

"I have to, Crowhurst, otherwise I should not be here."

"Where would you be, sir?"

"Still in the stork's nest. Tell me, Crowhurst, how long is it from conception to delivery?"

Crowhurst measured his diagram carefully with a ruler. "About eight inches, sir."

"We're not on Geography, Crowhurst. You know damn well what I mean."

"Oh, about nine months, sir except in my case. I was premature. Couldn't wait to get cracking, sir. Ha, ha, ha, ha! Where shall I put the placenta, sir?"

"On your head. There is an old midwives' tale that it curdles the brain."

Crowhurst was an odd mixture of precocity and clown, whereby he served up strange answers in the examinations. Asked to define a gentleman in the English paper he wrote: 'A gentleman is a man who gives up his seat to a lady in a public convenience'. In the History paper he wrote: Archaeologists have proved beyond doubt that Stone Age Man suffered from rheumatism because they have dug up their knobbly knees'.

"I expect it will please you to hear what I'm making for my CSE project in Craft, sir. I'm sculpturing a life-size model of the female reproductive system in clay and plastic, sir."

"Why the devil can't you make bookcases or steam-engines like normal boys?"

"Because my friend Nigel Beaumont is sculpturing a lifesize model of the male reproductive system, sir. You see, sir, our class had to pair off and design objects which were complementary to one another, like interlocking space-stations or sectional bookcases. So Nigel and me designed Fred and Deb. That's why we have to work from a blue print to be dead accurate, sir."

"Do you mean to tell me your teacher has passed it?"

"I don't think so, sir. He's only just had a little daughter."

"I mean permitted it, idiot."

"Ah, we assured him Fred and Deb are married, sir—that's why she's preggers. So they've got to fit within a tolerance of one thou on the micrometer, sir. I'll show you Marigold who's going to slide into the womb upside down. I knocked her off of my little sister, sir, but she's the right size."

Crowhurst produced a doll from a plastic wrapper in his duffel bag, appropriately nude for her role as Foetus Mark One, according to the label he had gummed to her bottom.

"When are you going to show us the VD film strip, sir? I hear it's pretty juicy, all in colour with giant ulcers like volcano craters, sir."

I had already vetted the film strip, which was extremely frank and earthy, sparing us nothing in its huge blow-ups of how to recognize one's new condition. As each frame was screened I was expected to read from a booklet a running commentary explaining the fleshy panorama on view and the medical story behind it, rather like a courier passing through the Swiss Alps with a party of apprentice mountaineers. Also included were some lurid shots of Soho strip joints and other shady rendezvous under the general heading of Where to Get It. The teacher who had shown the film to Nigel Beaumont's group told me that Nigel's study notes contained the names of all these entertainment houses, including a massage parlour, and that Nigel had requested the teacher to organize a school trip to London that the class might see for themselves the dangers to be avoided.

"I believe your friend Beaumont has already noted down the information you require, Crowhurst," I replied coldly.

"Have you ever been inside a strip club, sir?"

"Of course not, lad."

"Then how do you manage to describe them so accurately in your books, sir?"

"I . . . er . . . read about them, then make it up."

"I didn't know teachers read naughty books, sir."

"They do not, Crowhurst."

"My Dad does, sir."

"You shock me."

"Yes, sir, he reads *Sex International* but I don't expect you've ever heard of that one."

"I should hope not, Crowhurst."

"That's what I told him, sir, when he showed me a story in it all about Soho written by you, sir."

"Ah, did he now? Purely an imaginative piece, believe me."

"She certainly was, sir. Beaumont and me was wondering if you could get her to come and talk to the class about her job for our Careers Project, sir."

"Oh my God!" The profanity jumped unbidden from my lips as I sweated under cross-examination during this object lesson in how to hold the attention of a class. My mind's eye saw me introducing Babs to Dr Collins—'We've been fortunate to secure the services of Miss O'Connor, the celebrated trampoline dancer and body vibrator, to address our Careers Forum on Working in London After Dark. Miss O'Connor assures me her talk will be of particular interest to girls who like meeting people, helping others, variety, plenty of exercise and £100 a week'.

"Please, sir, have you ever seen a blue film?" This was Crowhurst's idea of changing the subject to save me from further embarrassment in front of the class.

"I hope teachers are not in the habit of frequenting such places, Crowhurst."

"Beaumont and me have, sir."

"A typical family evening round the home projector with your Dad, I presume?—'And now kiddies, let's see what really happened to Snow White when the Seven Dwarfs tired of whistling'."

"No, sir, me and Beaumont sneaked into the Thrillorama last

Saturday night."

"But the Thrillorama is a members-only cinema, Crowhurst, for showing those dreadful uncensored films to . . . er, well . . . to members."

"I know, sir, but me and Beaumont climbed in through the bog window, then sneaked into the seats under cover of gunfire —when they kill everybody in the church with tommyguns. Six hundred I think it was, sir, all singing *Bless this House.* So no one saw us, sir, because they was gasping bug-eyed at the white church turning red in technicolor and heads sticking to the walls like gargoyles. I liked the way half the preacher fell out of the pulpit and half of him hit the organ pipes."

It occurred to me how, years ago, I was allowed to take Hilda Longbothem to the cinema on the strict understanding we came out after the Donald Duck cartoon, that she might not be exposed to the horrors of *Mrs Minniver* or *Kind Hearts and Coronets.*

"I think we've had enough violence for one day, Crowhurst. Let's get on with our work, eh?"

"But you said you wanted discussion points, sir. You said free discussion was essential in modern education. You said everything must be brought out into the open to purify it, sir. You said. . . ."

"Point taken, Crowhurst, so let us discuss football for a change."

"There was a football match in the big picture, sir, where she picked up men at the end of the game. . . . What a film, sir— it had the lot. It was called *Have this one on me, Cheri,* all about a French nympho. But I could understand most of it without the subtitles."

"I bet you could."

"If we had a film like that in our Language Department, sir, we wouldn't half pass out in French."

"You wouldn't be the only one to pass out either." Once

93

again I saw myself telling Dr Collins, 'Another breakthrough in our Language Laboratory, sir—a French documentary about personal relationships and how a woman can help her fellow men. Yes sir, the class is interested and well attended—just over one thousand pupils in there for Period Six inmmediately after break. Yes sir, they've been in there all day, and some of our absentees have returned to school at last. Sorry, Dr Collins, but you cannot go in yourself because it's members only—oh, excuse me a moment while I assist the staff to carry Madame Monteux through to the sick room'.

"Now let us drop the whole distasteful subject, Crowhurst, so you can get on with your sectional pelvises," I suggested. Crowhurst plagued my life with this sort of routine, combing the books I wrote for ammunition like a Russian censor checking *Mein Kampf.*

"But I was just coming to the interesting bit, sir."

"Not in front of the girls, eh, Crowhurst?"

"No, sir, I mean about Beaumont spotting your name in the credits. You wrote the English subtitles, sir. Beaumont and me felt reelly proud about that, sir."

I gave Crowhurst the smile I so often had to give him— one of bland embarrassment at being caught red-handed, such as a judge might register when caught picking the prisoner's pocket. "Ah, that was long ago, lad. You see, a writer has to scrape a living the best he can in many fields."

"Last year isn't long ago, sir. I managed to spot the date of the film right at the bottom, where it says in small print 'Copyright Erotic Art Productions Inc., MDCMLXXIII'. I expect they always give the date of the film in Roman numerals so it won't seem so old when it is put on telly."

"But you must understand that a film takes ages to make sometimes years." I said this in a tone which implied that *Have This One On Me, Cheri* could well have started out on magic-lantern slides lit by an oil-lamp. English subtitles and dubbing

94

dialogue had been the most frustrating of all my literary career, struggling to provide words for audiences who did not care what the players said so long as they did it. I learned to translate long speeches as 'My husband does not understand me' and short speeches as 'Darling!' or 'Happy?' Mostly the characters were neurotic, humourless lovers who barked at each other in monosyllables between cigarettes, often glancing through bedroom windows of village *maisons* to see if someone they hated was coming back unexpectedly or early or late. There was a lot of 'Gaston suspects us,' 'My wife is away', and innumerable short sharp, '*Peut-êtres*!' followed by a heavy silence while they lit more cigarettes.

As a creative writer there wasn't much I could do with all those *Peut-êtres* which they snapped out as though trying to shorten the word Potato. I experimented with translating it as Perhaps! Perhaps? Per . . . haps—even Maybe for a change, but it made no difference because they invariably ended up in bed, when my services were not required until I had to pop up with 'Cigarette?' 'Yes.' 'Happy?' 'Perhaps.'

"This film couldn't have taken years to make, sir, because the baby in it didn't change size one bit."

"A simple film tack, Crowhurst—we got through seven babies during production."

"But none of the actors got older, sir."

"Clever make-up. Note how one lady of the town walks her beat in a wheel-chair towards the end."

"Anyway, sir, Nigel and me were jolly proud of you as a writer like that. But what we really want to see is the one you acted in, sir—*Rose Loathes Clothes.* When that comes back to the Thrillorama could you take the whole class to see it in the afternoon as part of our course, sir?"

Now I was really in trouble, practising physical shrinkage as the implications hit me. As a young actor in search of his Hamlet I had unwittingly signed up for one of the early health-through-starkers girlie films in which I was the nude prude who walked about the beach wearing only the *Daily Mirror* until fifteen maidens started a waste-paper drive that necessitated my lying flat on the sands, praying for the tide to come in.

"Most cinemas do cheap rates for school parties, sir," Crowhurst advised me, and once again my mind's eye saw me telling Dr Collins the glad tidings: 'I am taking 4a to see *Rose Loathes Clothes* at the Thrillorama this afternoon, Dr Collins. It is the visual follow-up in our project on Birth, Marriage and Old Age—actually this documentary film covers the health aspect of our lives, sir, emphasizing the importance of sunshine on our bodies and the harmful effects of wearing clothes. For example, when the missionaries first put Aborigine women into dresses they developed pneumonia. No, sir, the women did, not the missionaries. This film will be of particular value to the class because I myself happen to be taking part in the therapeutic callisthenics sequences known as strip volleyball, played without the handicap of unhealthy garments or the repressive segregation of the sexes. *Mens Sana in Corpore Sano,* sir, a healthy mind in a healthy body—with particular reference to the latter. What will especially appeal to your good self, sir, is that we can get in at 25p per head as a school party at the matinee, including the live Go-Go dancer on stage during the intermission—a Miss Ophelia Nockers is the artiste's name I believe—followed by Take Your Partners Please for an Old-Tyme Orgy at the Thrillorama social club'.

Crowhurst aimed his buck teeth at me with a satisfied smirk. "Please sir, why are you sweating? Don't you feel well?"

"It is oppressively hot in here, Crowhurst, nothing more."

Crowhurst checked the classroom thermometer with the intensity of one suffering from extreme myopia. "68 degrees Fahrenheit, sir, quite a comfortable room temperature. What would that be in Centigrade, sir?"

"I have no idea—and care less."

"Let me see, sir, F minus 32, times 5, divided by 9, equals 20. 20 degrees Centigrade, sir—does that make it any better? Or I should say 20 degrees Celsius, as invented by Anders Celsius of Sweden. I wonder when he invented that, sir?"

"I don't know. I should know so I'll look it up for you after school."

"1742, sir. Wouldn't it be interesting to find out which came first, sir, Celsius or Fahrenheit?"

"Fascinating problem."

"Fahrenheit, sir. He was a German who invented his scale in 1726 on a mercury thermometer. See, sir, therm-meter, a measurer of heat."

"Why aren't you at Grarnmar School, Crowhurst?"

"Mr Mould says I should be, sir. He's moved heaven and earth to get me transferred. I'm a late developer, sir. Mr Mould told my mum that if the Local Education Authority won't shift me to Cudford Grammar School he may have to resign from teaching in protest, sir."

"I may be forced to follow suit."

"A lot of the staff say that, sir. They all want to see me get on, yet I don't really want to move because I like it here. Mr Mould has given me a great deal of encouragement, sir. He says Cudford Secondary Modern School doesn't really specialize in turning out nuclear physicists, so I would be better off anywhere else. What's more, he's promised to petition the Queen on my behalf. Do you think I shall have to visit Buckingham Palace, sir?"

"Only if you manage to escape from the Tower of London."

"What shall I say to her Majesty, sir?"

"Say 'I wonder how I managed to escape from the Tower of London, ma'am?'"

"No, I mean really, sir. What shall I say?"

"You'll say, 'Please, ma'am, I wonder what this lovely palace cost before John Nash redesigned it in 1825?' Then the

Queen will say, 'I hear that you want to go to Grammar School, young man,' and you'll reply, 'George the Third bought it in 1760 for £21,000, your Majesty'."

"1761, sir."

"Then the Queen will ask you about your school career and you'll reply 'A new wing was added in 1846, ma'am, then the ballroom was built in 1856. I wonder how big the ballroom is, your Majesty?' She will hint politely that it is almost large enough to get your head in, whereupon you will answer, '111 feet by 60 feet, ma'am'. Then the Queen will inquire graciously about your parents and if they have gone off their rockers yet, so you will reassure her with, 'Sir Aston Webb designed the beautiful new front of the palace, ma'am. I wonder when he done that?' But now you find yourself alone in the audience chamber, so you have to shout after her at the top of your voice, 'He done it in 1913, ma'am . . . HE DONE IT IN 1913! I wonder what happened the following year? Come back, your Majesty, and hear all about the Great War up to 1918 before you go to Sandringham. I WONDER WHO BUILT SANDRINGHAM IN 1869. . .?'"

I checked myself abruptly, suddenly realizing I was shouting inordinately. Then I heard a voice calling up from the playground below. It said, "I believe it was Queen Victoria who built Sandringham." Going to the window I discovered Dr Collins looking up to me with a puzzled expression on his face, but before I could offer an explanation Crowhurst was calling down over my shoulder, "No, sir, not Queen Victoria. It was King Edward the Seventh when he was still Prince of Wales."

"Just having a lively historical discussion with the class, Dr Collins," I explained, only to find myself addressing an empty playground.

"What colour shall I do the male scrotum, sir?" Linda asked me as I turned round.

"Try lilac," I suggested absent-mindedly.

SIX

I sought out Mr Mould in the staff room to question him about Crowhurst, only to find him reciting the Teacher's Prayer—a copy of which he had pinned to the notice-board. It ran like this: 'Preserve us this day from all child psychiatrists, cranky College lecturers, Headmistresses on horseback, crackpot teachers, promotion charlies, do-gooders, education experts, professors of paediatrics, potty parents, comedy writers, and all other persons who do not understand children. Forgive our own Headmaster because he is comparatively harmless.'

I heard Mr Mould mutter, "Now I must add myself to the list, though I never thought I should live to see such a thing."

"What is the trouble, Mr Mould?" I inquired, sensing his agitation and remembering our motto that a trouble shared is a trouble doubled.

Mr Mould puffed furiously at his pipe, holding up some letters for my inspection. "Listen to this, Pook. 'Sorry Bob was absent from school yesterday but he had to get a haircut for the fishing competition.' And this, 'Philip is a Select Angel of Detroit now, so he must not bring home raffle tickets, act in Christmas plays or do anything religious. Please do not mention Easter to him'."

"Some parents can be difficult, Mr Mould."

"Difficult? This one's damn-nigh impossible. Listen: 'Dear Mr Mould, I don't want Mary taught Biology, Art, Religious Knowledge or anything else not directly connected with her career. PE and Games are a waste of time, too, so cut it out. What good is Science and History to a girl? All she needs is English and Maths."

"What does she want to do when she finishes school?"

"Leave home, I should think. Which reminds me of my own daughter, Pook. She's twenty now and going to be married."

Petra was extremely clever, with fourteen O-levels and three

A-levels, but she had been a disappointment to her father because she worked in a fishmonger's and dressed like Queen Victoria at bedtime. She had fallen in love with a hirsute gentleman we thought was in his seventies, but it seemed he was only twenty-four. He was so bearded that Petra must have found it almost impossible to kiss him; in fact, Mr Mould wondered if his daughter had experienced an aberration in her sex instincts and fallen in love with a bush. Francis never spoke, though Petra declared he did converse with her when alone, and Mr Mould believed he maintained this silence in order to husband his strength for such arduous tasks as standing up or lifting Petra's money onto the bar for drinks. Francis was indeed very thin, as though his parents had been over-protective and not told him about food until it was too late.

"The vicar may have to come out of the church and marry Francis in the taxi outside," Mr Mould mused. "He'll never make it to the altar on foot."

"Have they found somewhere to live, Mr Mould?" I inquired.

Mr Mould laughed mirthlessly. "Oh yes. He intends living with his parents, and Petra will live with us. She says nothing matters so long as they are wed. She broke this news to me when I said how sorry I shall be to lose her. After the courtship I've been subjected to, it seems the only person I shall lose is my son-in-law—he's practically lived with us up to now.'

"Suppose they both move in with you?"

"Mrs Mould has threatened to leave home if they do, so every cloud has a silver lining. This is the one thing I like about Francis—my wife can't stand the sight of him. She calls him the thin red loin."

"Where will they spend the honeymoon, Mr Mould?"

"Well, it's supposed to be a secret, but I think it will be in the waiting-room on Cudford Station. That's the only thing they've managed to save up for. Petra thinks their marriage will have a better chance if they don't live together. She says that's where my wife and I went wrong. However, she will still continue to call for Francis and take him out in the evenings."

"What happens if they have a baby, Mr Mould?"

"Assuming it survives birth in a bus shelter Petra will give it to us while she goes out to work the following day. Then we shall all visit Francis in Cudford Hospital."

"This must be a great disappointment to you, Mr Mould."

"That is why I am including myself in the Teacher's Prayer. I had expected a lot of Petra—my wife taught her to cook so that her hands are quite gnarled with opening tins. I taught her good husbandry to the extent that she's even found a use for broken light-bulbs. But what really worries me is her wedding dress. Because it's so elaborate that she looks as if she's muffled up to face an English summer. It costs £50, so she's been going round to her men friends saying, 'Will anybody buy me for £50? I'm yours for half-a-ton. Who wants me for ten fives?'"

"Where did you go wrong, Mr Mould?"

"I trace it back to the night I first met her mother in an air-raid shelter."

"Plenty of men met their wives in air-raid shelters though."

"But not when the war was gone and forgotten. I am reminded of little Sandra MacLean's essay last week in which she states: 'Soon after my mum and dad got married they had a budgie'. I think that is what happened to us."

Little Sandra MacLean was the sweet twelve-year-old lassie who had come on at the school concert dressed in full tartan, smiled nervously in the silence of the hall, then suddenly blasted us out of our seats with an explosion of bagpipes, like having an ambulance siren go off in one's bedroom at dawn. Poor Mrs Collins had been caught unawares with her hearing-aid on full volume and had to be treated for shock in the medical room. It seemed impossible that such a little girl could produce such power without electronic amplification but she maintained it for eight minutes, while the audience sat there unashamedly blocking their ears against the onslaught of *Amazing Grace,* followed without warning by *Doon in the Glen,* which caught some of us with our fingers out. Mr Mould had remarked afterwards that nothing would induce him to enter a Scottish glen now, and he would be found terror-stricken and dazed up a Scottish highland.

We were interrupted by the dramatic entry of Mrs Crust from the Arts and Craft. Mrs Crust threw herself into a chair with a harrowing appeal for aspirins. I hurried to my locker, where I kept a large bottle of Teaching Aids, as we called Boots' pain relievers, for the benefit of our staff. Miss Shampoo fetched a glass of water for her sister in distress and sighed sympathetically. Miss Shampoo—who suffered much under the burden of such a name despite her protestations that she was of Burmese descent and resented her nickname of Dandruff—also knew what pain was because she was struggling to teach History without text-books. Her predecessor—Miss, now Professor, Nuneaton—had purged the school of history books by crating them up and despatching them as far away as possible to emerging Africa in order to cleanse us from bias and to induce us to the Nuneaton New Approach to History, a system which was hard to put your finger on except that the pupils went out of school with work-sheets on clip-boards and ended up in Marty's Coffee Bar. When unable to go out, the children appeared to re-enact old battles and industrial riots in the classroom, wherefrom we heard authentic commands and battle cries ringing round the block from Miss Nuneaton, such as "Shut up, you little devils or I'll fetch the Head!"

Nevertheless, Miss Nuneaton's exciting new methods gained her promotion as History Adviser to Cudford County Council, but her departure left Miss Shampoo a History syllabus without a book in the stock-cupboard. Nothing, in fact, except a set of clip-boards, a map of Cudford, a shovel, two sieves and a bucket containing torn-up work-sheets. This state of affairs had left Miss Shampoo so short of temper that Mr Mould said she would stop Oscar Wilde in mid-epigram and tell him not to be rude.

Mrs Crust's daily appeal for aspirins and a shotgun was inspired by the new Arts and Craft block, which had abandoned the traditional classroom, leaped over the modern open-plan design and had introduced us to the futuristic landscaped teaching zone. This meant that in place of four classrooms we now possessed a vast area for the four teachers and their 120 pupils, which, to quote Mrs Crust, was like working in a steel plant during a thunderstorm. The teachers communicated with the pupils by means of sign language, except when Mr Whittle was using the power tools and everybody's hands were required as ear-muffs.

Mrs Crust's nerves had become so frayed that when she put a formal protest to the Head in writing he had suggested we use her letter as a spelling correction test for the pupils. Dr Collins told her how fortunate she was to have the new landscaped teaching zone, and made the surprising statement that because it did not have the traditional dividing walls it cost a lot more money. He did not react kindly to Mr Mould's suggestion that we ask the builders to put in old-fashioned walls and give us a cash rebate, emphasizing that nothing could be changed at this late stage and that the builders were fully employed in discovering why the exterior walls were cracking before the formal opening of the block by the Mayor. Mr Mould hinted there was some danger of the Mayor tugging the curtain cord to unveil the plaque and pulling that side of the building down on top of him. He saw the press headline as: 'Mayor buried alive at opening ceremony. He pulled cord too hard says contractor of demolished school.'

Frankly, we had been suspicious of County Architects for same time because their design for traffic flow in school seemed to be based on rush hour in the Japanese train service at Tokyo, where special porters are employed to shoulder passengers in so they can shut the doors. This was best exemplified in my teaching block at the convergence of four classrooms, where, on the bell, 160 children had to leave through 160 children waiting to enter. For this explosion of 320 pupils the architects had provided a corridor only six feet wide, known to us as the mincer, and to the boys as the tunnel of love.

"Take your partners please, ladies and gentlemen, for an old-time mass suicide," Mrs Crust gasped as she sank the aspirins. "I know what they mean now by Art can only express itself through suffering, but I'm too young to die in the name of lino-cuts and fabric-printing. Rush me to the Ladies' loo so I can paint The Flood on the ceiling in peace."

Miss Shampoo gave us her drawn look of mankind in anguish. "I am extremely worried about little Gerald Sloper," she informed us tragically. "He is a nice, good-mannered boy, smartly dressed and well spoken."

"What's he doing here then?" Mr Mould inquired. "Under the 1944 Education Act he is expressly forbidden."

"Where have we gone wrong?" I asked.

"Unfortunately, because of being backward, Gerald is in a remedial form, where he is in danger of corruption by our . . . er . . . ne'er-do-wells and less able children from deprived homes."

"Stop!" Mr Mould cried dramatically. "Miss Shampoo, I must warn you not to introduce class barriers into our staff room. The experts have been at pains to impress upon us that they do not exist, and, what is more, we must get rid of them immediately."

"But Gerald's parents, who coach the boy at home, have been to see me and pleaded for our help in removing him from the adverse environment which he himself detests. He does not like stealing, swearing, vandalism, disorder, apathy and smoking which surrounds him."

"Has he seen the County psychiatrist?"

"I have had to explain to them that I can do nothing. Only in an examination stream will he be better off, but he could not possibly cope with the work. Because he tries so hard he is unpopular with his classmates, some of whom have beaten him up for it."

Mr Mould puffed his pipe and stretched across the table for the County Educational Bulletin. "I refer you, of course, to Professor Nuneaton of treasured memory, Miss Shampoo. Her current article states categorically that such a situation does not exist and it is our fault that it does. Listen : 'Teachers must stop inflicting corporal punishment on defenceless children and locking them up in classroom prisons away from the excitement of the streets. Above all, they must stop erecting artificial class barriers which do not exist . . .' and so on. Now here is a lady who, were she to write about sweeping chimneys, would probably begin: 'Employers must stop young children of seven being sent up chimneys to sweep them'."

"Or 'When will the Admiralty abandon sail in favour of steam-driven paddle-wheels?'" I suggested.

"This, of course, is the Aunt Sally technique favoured by some experts, such as: 'Teachers must stop erecting a barrier between the children and the facts of life'. My answer to that is little Malcolm Fowl's essay here. Malcolm is eleven years and ten months old but the opening line of his essay would not seem to suggest a very high barrier has been erected to protect him from the facts of life: 'Gary loves all the girls because he is a sex maniac and he loves all the men because he is an Omo'."

"Maybe it's the staff who are over-protected, Mr Mould. When Miss Crossley heard her form were playing strip-poker she said, 'Oh dear, I do hope the poor things won't take cold'."

Just then Karen approached me, all wide-eyed, soft lipped and head on one side, like women do when they want something more from you. Karen possessed the ability to be more female than is fair under the genetic code, rather like boxing an opponent who squares up to you in the ring with three arms, so I thanked my lucky stars she could not twist me round her finger as though I was the usual run of men. She tried the old trick of holding both my hands as if preparing a small seance for two, then parted her lips, giving me the odd sensation that we were in bed together standing up. I had been very concerned lately about this odd sensation when I spoke to Karen or Rosalind— in fact, only yesterday when the school bell rang I said to Rosalind absent-mindedly, "Time to get up, darling," and she gave me the strangest look. Even in the Bold Forester when buying a pint from Shirley the barmaid I experienced this hal- lucination, especially when she reached up to the whisky optic to show us her long legs, then parked her bust on the counter for a chat. Not that this bothered me, except that the alcohol seemed to reverse the effect of the tablets I was on and I found myself trying to blow out the ornamental electric candle beside us.

Karen spoke with shining eyes. "Peter, I want you to come horse-riding with me," she announced.

"Oh joy!" I had long discovered the uncanny bond between horses and me, whereby they sensed instinctively that my object was to lie stunned between their hoofs while they smelt my crumpled body. All except the mare who had taken me for a walk through a beautiful Indian forest, stopping only when we emerged from the trees that I might admire the view. I sat there petrified on the lip of a gorge nine hundred feet deep, staring unbelievingly at the piece of string far below which was a mighty river The mare's head was actually in space beyond the edge of this massive crack in the earth's crust, as if I was sitting on the back of a resting eagle instead of a horse. It was the first time in my life I reversed the usual process and threw myself off a horse, employing the unorthodox back somersault technique over her rump and crawled to safety.

I had also been taken for a gallop across the South African veld by a black stallion, who, sensing I desired excitement, swerved at the last moment to avoid a twenty-foot rock, thus leaving me still in the jockey position but minus a horse, to hit the rock six feet above ground level. They told me afterwards that parts of my wreckage were strewn over a wide area, like a plane crash, and my watch had been located in a distant gully.

"I want you to come with me on the Exmoor Expedition," Karen begged.

"What on earth for, dear?"

"So we can be alone together for a whole week, Peter."

"On Exmoor!" I was strictly a city hunter who had always found the great outdoors most unnatural and artificial. My experiences round the world had convinced me how beautiful it was, but that Nature only showed you the beauty to take your mind off dying from hunger and exposure—a kind of healthy grave, as Sydney Smith described it.

"Just think how happy we'd be up there," Karen persisted, as though referring to Heaven. "You and me alone together!"

"You might as well say how happy we'd be together on the rack. What's wrong with comfortable old-fashioned here?"

"Well, for one thing, I don't fancy being alone with Mr Whittle and eighty kids. You see, there's got to be a woman teacher for the girls."

"Whittle and eighty kids on Exmoor, plus horses! You must be joking, Karen. Torture was forbidden in this country around 1640. I'd sooner attend a Teacher's Union Conference."

"Won't you please come for my sake, Peter?" How did she make her eyes moist at the drop of a hat, like some people can waggle their ears?

"It's for your sake I'm not coming, dear. I don't want a woman to witness me murdering Whittle with my bare hands in his own cave."

"So you would protect me, dear?"

"No, dear, women don't need protecting from men. This would be merely a ritual sacrifice in the evening to amuse the children in place of television. I'm sorry, Karen, but it's just not on—and that's final."

Sometimes a man has to be cruel to be kind, even if it means breaking a woman's heart.

I crouched behind a tree, down-wind and some three hundred yards to the lee of the camp. Not a soul to be seen, so I opened a Benson and Hedges packet and lit up, feeling quite dizzy as the nicotine hit me. I was down-wind lest Mr Whittle should snake his head into the air and scent the breeze like a gazelle with twitching nostrils, and alone lest the children should scream "Pollution, pollution, pollution!" as though my cigarette smoke was blotting out Exmoor under a mighty blanket of black fumes.

I was full of peppermint sweets I had to chew continuously to conceal the fact that I smoked and drank secretly from the rest of the party, who could detect my sins at long range in the pure air of Exmoor. I was fed up with fourteen-year-old girls sniffing me all day long for signs of pollution and breaking the no-smoking rule Mr Whittle had laid down for all.

Worse still, I was in disgrace and barred from horse-riding. The previous day I had sat in the staff latrine having a cigarette, feeling that this was the only place for a bit of privacy, if only behind four sides of sackcloth with no top. I had only to raise my head a foot or so to ensure there was nobody about to give me away. Eventually I threw the cigarette butt into the chemical toilet, whereupon something went *pomp* quite loudly and flames shot up from the toilet, surrounding me on three sides.

Screaming with pain I ran outside, yet even then remembering the first-aid manual recommended holding a burnt finger under a tap to dissipate the heat. Without hesitation I made for our sole water supply, the static water tank, and sat in it with my legs over the edge. From this position I was able to watch the staff latrine send a great column of smoke and flame into the Exmoor sky as it burnt to the ground. At that moment it did not worry me because I felt certain there were third-degree burns where I had been caught like an egg in an egg-cup.

Whittle and the others ran from their tents upon hearing the chemical closet finally blow up. Whittle could not grasp the connection between the explosion and my sitting with my rear in the static water tank.

"Don't use that water tank, you maniac!" he shrieked. "What do you think the latrines are for? Do you want everyone to go down with typhoid?"

"I'm badly burned," I howled, pointing to the fire. "The staff latrine has exploded."

"Haven't you the sense to use the pupils' latrine, idiot!"

I lost my temper. "I'm not using any latrine, Whittle—I'm trying to save my buttocks. The closet caught fire under me."

"Where is it, man?"

"It was there, where the bushes are still burning. It's a miracle I'm not dead."

"Good God, if that reaches our tents it'll burn down the whole camp. Pull your trousers up and help me beat it out. Fire drill, everybody! Find anything you can lay your hands on and beat out the flames."

The children fell to with a will, but I did not stir. I figured that if they rushed me to Taunton Hospital I might be saved, then later they could graft skin from my face onto my backside. Moreover, I had a premonition that my love life was finished.

After the panic had died down I had to lie on my stomach in the tent for examination — by Karen, who was in charge of first-aid, and by Whittle, who was furious at the loss of his precious closet.

"This will look a pretty kettle of fish in my report to Dr Collins," Whittle fumed.

"Why don't you photograph it in colour for him," I suggested.

"I happen to be referring to our portable latrine, not the recumbent one before me, Pook. I'm charging you with deliberately throwing a lighted cigarette into the chemicals."

"But that would be against the rules, Whittle."

"Are you so naive as to suggest that you sat on a camp toilet and it exploded under you by self-combustion? Rubbish, man. You have been violating the rules ever since we left Cudford. Well, for a start, I am banning you from the pony trek."

I laughed mirthlessly. "That won't break my heart, seeing that it is unlikely I shall ever be able to sit down again."

"Instead, you will lead the walk across Exmoor with the group of children for whom there are no horses."

"That will be difficult from the intensive care unit of the hospital."

"Listen to me, Pook, it is quite obvious from here that your posterior is somewhat scorched and as red as a box of tomatoes, but your revolting action of immersing it in the water tank has saved you from serious injury. Furthermore, Karen's devoted treatment is all that you require."

"But there's not a hair left on my body."

"Which I trust will teach you not to flout the no-smoking rule again. How is our wayward patient, Nurse Dewar?'

"Och, he'll do fine," Karen laughed, delighted to have a victim to practise on. "By way of experiment I'm treating his left buttock with tannic acid jelly, and his right one with acriflavine emulsion in liquid paraffin, so we'll see which gets better first. Then I'm treating his more sensitive parts with a warm solution of picric acid."

"Picric acid!" I gasped, horrified by the implications.

"And if any blisters form I shall nip them with my sterilized scissors. Above all, Peter, you mustn't get cold."

"Cold! Are you sure I'm not alight at the back, Karen?"

"No, Peter, you're just a wee bittie saire, so dinna fash yersel' th' noo."

Despite the pain I recalled how Karen tended to break into dialect when amorously excited, and I hoped she would not expect me to reciprocate. A dentist hardly expects his patient to kiss him as the teeth come out.

"Perhaps I should stay with him during the night," Karen said to Mr Whittle in her hospital voice.

"Why, do you think he will attempt to set fire to his paraffin dressings?" Whittle smirked.

"Well, he has experienced rather a severe shock."

"And I don't want another one during the night," I cried. "I'll be quite all right, honestly."

I felt sexless and extremely vulnerable, lying there half naked on my stomach. I was convinced that my buttocks had swollen to such dimensions that they filled the tent like two enormous observatory domes, and that before long they would burst the tent from its moorings so that it would become a mere tarpaulin, like the carpet over the back of a ceremonial elephant. In the darkness I imagined wayfarers mistaking me for Dunkery Beacon, and the white hot glow luring mariners to destruction along the coast.

Karen returned after lights out at ten-thirty to announce her intention of sitting up with me. I asked her if I might have a cigarette, whereupon she replied that if I was good and did as she wanted there might be one later on, and that if I tried to forget my injuries and continued to behave well she would then consider giving me a match to light it too. On the other hand, if I played up I would get her hand across my backside as hard as possible and no fag.

As I endeavoured to sort out Karen's code of reward and punishment, she suddenly announced her intention of turning in for the night.

I felt more than relieved at the news. "Cheerio, Karen. Thanks for everything and see you in the morning. Could you leave me a fag before you go?"

For reply she snuggled up by my side and kissed me. "I am a woman, Peter," she informed me in that whisper girls adopt when making factual statements sound like revelations of science. "Have you forgotten I am a woman, Peter?"

"No, dear, I keep saying to myself 'Karen is a woman'."

"What is more, Peter, I am a real woman—a man's woman."

"Let's hope your man doesn't find you in here with me, then."

"Do you know what I want more than anything else in the world tonight, Peter?"

"The gift of healing?"

"No, Peter, I mean concerning men."

"One that can move without pain?"

"Ah, I am going to help you forget your pain tonight, Peter."

"A fag at last."

"You see, Peter, I thought that when we were alone together on Exmoor everything would be different."

"It's a delicate subject, Karen, but I'm different for a start. I'm burnt out, as one might say."

"Love will find a way, darling."

"Like the Eskimoes; we can rub noses—at least there's no dressing on that."

"If you can turn onto your side, Peter, you'd be able to take me in your arms."

"I'll try, but you will have to take me in your arms—even blinking my eyes seems to stretch the skin round my bottom."

I lay in Karen's soft embrace feeling like a charred corpse, in the most embarrassing predicament of my life. She kissed me and gently felt my dressings, so that I lay in fear that she would resort to the sterilized scissors mentioned in her first-aid book.

"How do you feel now, darling?" she whispered.

"Very, very tired, Karen. I guess it's the reaction. I'll probably fall asleep in your arms right now."

"Excellent—I'll just give you a couple of analgesics to kill any more pain."

Karen gave me two tablets, but I thought it odd that she took them, not from the school medical chest, but from her handbag. She also let me have a cigarette, saying I had been a good boy so far but I could have one anyway. This too I could not resolve. I had been so deprived of tobacco to keep Exmoor unpolluted that the nicotine went straight to my head, so I must needs lay it on Karen's bosom and smoke from the corner of my mouth with closed eyes. I pictured Mr Whittle's nostrils twitching in his sleep two tents down the line, like certain moths can locate their mate half-a-mile distant.

"Has the pain gone, Peter?" Karen inquired as she stubbed out the butt for me.

"Yes, dear, the pain has gone, but something new has arrived." I said this quite calmly to conceal from her the power with which the sap of life was rising in my veins, as though the red deer of Exmoor were calling me to rut week. I wondered what Karen's reaction would be if she realized she was nursing in her arms the bull of the herd.

"You've gone very hot, dear," Karen exclaimed, feeling my brow.

"So will you in a minute if I don't cool down. Are you sure those tablets you gave me weren't for the horses?" I have never completely trusted women since childhood, when I stole some chocolates from Aunt Mabel's sideboard. The next time I took some I was confined to the toilet for forty-eight hours suffering from what we used to call the galloping pants-down.

"Of course not, Peter. Why?"

"Because I have an overwhelming sensation of the chess player who is about to move his bishop to mate."

"Why you fruity old thing, Peter!"

"I want to make it quite clear, Karen, that if you have taken advantage of my condition to pill me up for your own ends I shall never forgive you. . . ."

"Oh, don't sound so pompous, Peter."

"It's no laughing matter—the fighter primates were not born to mate and die, like male ants."

"Oh come here, yew wee Sassenach monster. . . !"

As Karen squeezed me for an action replay of Bannockburn my scream of agony echoed round the camp, bringing Mr Whittle running in with his torch and camp riot baton at the ready. He had often emphasized at his briefings that our camp was particularly vulnerable with so many girls in our charge, and had hinted that danger might not necessarily come from without, whereupon I had assured him of my complete trust in his personal integrity.

Mr Whittle stared unbelievingly at the sight which met his eyes—"My oath, Pook, you're attempting to seduce Miss Dewar! Thank heaven I heard her scream and arrived in time!"

"It was my scream, not hers," I protested indignantly.

"Spare us base lies, Pook. I know your little game. Miss Dewar kindly offers to sit up to nurse your burns, so you try to take advantage of her the moment my back is turned."

"It was largely my fault," Karen confessed.

Mr Whittle held up his hand in dramatic pose. "Please do not attempt to take any blame from his shoulders, Miss Dewar. I know you sat up with him as a nurse should, but you were not to suspect in what manner he would thank you for your solicitude. As he is obviously not to be trusted with the female sex and cannot ride a horse, I have decided in Daily Orders that tomorrow he shall lead the boys on the walk across Exmoor. You and I will lead the girls for the pony-trek—fortunately for all concerned, on an entirely different route."

"Walk across Exmoor!"

"Shut up, Pook! Come, Miss Dewar, I will escort you to your own tent, and we shall leave this reprobate to his thoughts."

I had received a strict Christian upbringing based on the precept of love thy neighbour and forgiving him, even if he owed you money—therefore I was a trifle surprised, as I had prayed for Whittle that he might not fall off his horse and break his neck tomorrow before I could get my hands on him and forgive him, to dream that Mr Whittle was lying at the foot of Dunkery Beacon disembowelled.

SEVEN

Crowhurst led the way because he knew all about orienteering, if he had not actually invented it. Furthermore, he was doing a project on Exmoor, which enabled him to explain the local ecology to me as we went along. He pointed out the Exmoor falcon hovering for its next victim, and I reflected that if we saw the Exmoor vulture I would unobtrusively bait Crowhurst's head with meat.

The burns made my progress painful, as though I had been wearing an eighteen-hour girdle for as many weeks, but I cheerfully joined with the others in singing *There's No Place Like Home.* We really had no option because the tune had been indelibly seared into our subconscious by Mr Donatello's icecream van which haunted the camp day and night, gradually transferring our pocket money from the tents to the van. The tune was played on a glockenspiel, sometimes halting in mid bar to indicate that Mr Donatello had caught another customer, then continuing to flood the site with electronic clarity. I had imagined Mr Donatello sitting in his van as he smote the glockenspiel with such monotonous regularity, but when I went to complain he was standing outside, accompanying the music in a sweet Italian tenor voice. He showed me the continuous tape which played the tune, and explained how, owing to the complex laws of copyright, another melody would double the cost of his ica-creamo.

Hence the entire camp sang, whistled or hummed *There's No Place Like Home* throughout the day and half the night, no matter what they might be doing. Mr Whittle tried to start a kind of swear-box, with a forfeit of a penny for singing it, but in vain because even as he took the box round he was humming the melody.

The beautiful scenery on the long gradual climb to the moor took our boys by surprise. Fred Rubble, who, despite being on free dinners and uniform allowance, visited the Continent twice yearly with his parents, made a striking comment: "I fought all the lovely views and all that was abroad sir. I didn't sort of fink we had nuffink like this 'ere, you know what I mean like?"

"I deduce your conclusion, Fred," I replied. "What puzzles me is the distant mirage, whereby the moors appear to be white instead of green."

"Snow, sir," Crowhurst informed us confidently.

"Snow in early summer?"

"Snow in late spring, sir. Three feet in places. Good thing we have our maps and compasses. More snow is forecast on the north wind blowing across the Bristol Channel, sir."

"Oh good." I said this to negate the inflection of bad news in Crowhurst's voice. Crowhurst liked to bring me bad news, or, even better, bad news followed by terrible news—like the time he led me to the book cupboard to view Linda Agate's body—apparently dead—then returned to tell me there had been a bomb warning and the school must be evacuated immediately.

"You'll be glad to know it's snowing now, sir, right here."

"Merely light sleet, Crowhurst."

"That's because we're nearing the snow-line, sir. Do you like snow, sir? I love it."

"I dread August when it is seldom recorded in Britain."

"Not since 1878, sir."

"1879, Crowhurst, 30th August, just before tea."

"Were you safely indoors, sir?"

"I happened to be sunbathing at Brighton, lying on top of the snowplough I always take on my summer holidays."

"Actually it was called Brighthelmstone then, sir."

Soon we were actually trudging through snow, and some of the boys were snowballing one another. A particularly well aimed missile hit me on the back of the neck—I say well aimed, but Crowhurst had crept up so close behind me that his glove almost touched my neck. I laughed sportingly to let the boys see

116

I enjoyed shock allied to discomfort, but what really concerned me just then was my equipment. My Polar boots purchased from Cudford Cash & Carry were designed on the principle of a ship's bilge to let water in, then out again. As for my Arctic anorak, the north wind went through it like a lady's petticoat, then through me and out the other side. My Everest woolly hat was most ingenious; the snow collected in the crown until my body heat melted it sufficiently to percolate through to cool my brain.

"River ahead, sir," Crowhurst called, locating the valley on his plastic-covered map. "We're in luck, sir, it's frozen over."

"So we can turn back and go home?"

"Oh no, sir. A chance to use our ice technique. Lie down on the ice, sir, with legs and arms wide to spread the weight, then we give you one big shove and across you go."

There is one snag about this ice technique; always ensure the river is frozen right across. Here there was still a narrow flow of water in the centre, which I mentioned to Crowhurst as I sank in it head-first. Fortunately, I did not panic because it is extremely difficult to panic when one is paralysed. Instead, I stood calmly upright in five feet of water, like a human stalagmite growing from the river bed. I learned by experiment that I could not even shout for help, and the sensation gripped me that I had fallen into the carbon dioxide outflow of an industrial refrigeration plant.

What I failed to understand was why Crowhurst was crying from the bank, "There's been an accident, sir!" I stared poker-faced at Crowhurst, unable to reply that if I lived there would be the worst accident Exmoor had ever known. Then I realized it must be his policy of bad news/terrible news—such as that I was just above the Victoria Falls and crocodiles had been sighted.

"There's been an accident, sir!" Crowhurst persisted. Surely he did not think I was so benumbed that I did not realize my plight? "Come quickly, sir—let the current take you down to the little bridge."

Bridge! Crowhurst knew there was a bridge, yet he had pushed me to my death flat on my stomach across thin ice. I discovered my eyeballs could still turn in my head, enabling me to discern a low wooden bridge down-stream—and I was drifting towards it like a frozen supermarket duck with ice-hard liver and kidneys packed inside. Or was I merely a bodiless head floating on the water? At least I was safe from hypothermia because hypothermia presupposed the presence of lowered body temperature, whereas in my condition a thermometer would simply shatter into fragments.

Many hands seized me at the bridge, dragging me clear of the water stiff as a plank, then violently massaged me all over.

"There's been an accident, sir," Crowhurst persisted, at the same time attempting to give me the kiss of life, during which operation his chewing-gum was fired down my larynx with considerable velocity. "Rubble laughed so much when you fell in the river, sir, that he wet hisself. What can we do about it, sir? There's no spare gear."

"Look what I done, sir," Rubble confirmed, standing astride me that I might see his jeans. "They're all sort of wet like, you know what I mean?"

I lay there on the bridge, frozen and waterlogged, marvelling yet again at children's remarkable order of priorities, whereby everybody's concern was for a damp patch on Rubble's jeans, while I was a dripping wreck soggy from total immersion.

"Camp," I gasped desperately. At the back of my mind was the thought that if we could regain our camp I could be rushed to the intensive care unit at Taunton, where they might be able to save my vital organs, particularly the kidneys which had turned to cold marble.

"All right, sir, but that's a long way just for a dry pair of jeans," Crowhurst remarked, giving orders for me to be hoisted up to see if I could walk if supported from either side. "Try to walk, sir, to restore the circulation, and don't worry any more about Rubble—it was his own silly fault for laughing at you."

After a mile or so, it occurred to me how strange it was that our journey back to base should be uphill instead of downhill, and that the snow was getting deeper. I put my problem to Crowhurst.

"Well, sir, it was very good of you to worry about Rubble, but the boys and me decided it was a pity to spoil our expedition just for him, so we voted to go on, sir. We're over half-way already and jolly good fun it is too, up here on top of the world, sir. By the way, sir, do you know what a white-out is?"

"I am about to know, Crowhurst."

"A white-out is what mountaineers dread most, next to avalanches."

"So that means we shall have a white-out, followed by an avalanche."

"Mountaineers dread a white-out because it snows so thick that you can't see the end of your nose, sir, and sometimes it's so bad that you don't realize you're being buried alive."

"Your attention has been diverted by the avalanche?"

"You can't see the avalanche, sir, only hear the roar as it engulfs you forever."

"Thank heaven we're not up a mountain then." I made a mental note never to go near so much as Highgate Hill with Crowhurst.

"Ah, but we could still have a white-out, sir."

"How?" It occurred to me I was more likely to have a black-out in my present mood.

"There, sir, coming across the Bristol Channel from the Welsh Mountains on the cruel north wind. Lucky we've got our maps and compasses, sir. Isn't is exciting?"

I peered northwards to a threatening sky ranging from black to white, almost as if the Welsh Mountains were moving across to Exmoor for Crowhurst's benefit so we could experience an avalanche as well as a white-out.

"What we need quickly is shelter, sir." Crowhurst predicted. "Preferably the one beneath Piccadilly Circus."

"Unfortunately, there isn't much around here, sir. I wouldn't want to be you, sir, responsible for the safety of forty boys on a barren uninhabited moor in a white-out."

"All right, Crowhurst, so that's the bad news. What's the terrible news?"

"We're lost, sir. Utterly and completely lost. Everything's covered in snow, but the map shows Exmoor in fine weather, so I couldn't check our landmarks, sir. No snow on the map, sir."

"Things might be worse, Crowhurst—you could have a brother."

"We're 1,200 feet up, sir, and lost somewhere in 265 square miles of National Park designated in 1954. . . ."

"Where's the track we're supposed to be following?"

"Right there, sir."

"I mean on the ground, idiot, not on the map."

"Ah, there's the rub, sir, if I may quote Hamlet, Act 3, because it's not snowing on the map like it is on the ground."

I gave Crowhurst a reassuring smile I copied from the Butcher Bird as it impales its prey on a thornbush. "Do the others suspect the danger we are in?"

"Oh yes, sir, I told everybody. No point in keeping it a secret up here, sir."

"Now you know the emergency drill—everybody must keep close together at all cost."

"Like a mass grave, sir? I read that the emperor penguins survive the Antarctic blizzards by forming an enormous circle with their backs to the snow, then gradually waddle in a kind of spiral so that everyone gets a turn in the middle."

"That's nonsense, Crowhurst. We are neither penguins nor are we in Antarctica."

"I can imitate a penguin, sir," Crowhurst replied, smiling at me with his buck teeth framed by those thick, unnaturally red lips.

"You look more like a walrus than a penguin."

Crowhurst began to waddle about, flapping his wings and jerking his head, then filling the air with a raucous cry—just as the snow hit us. It fell silently and heavily, as though we were at the bottom of a giant's flour mill, cutting down visibility to nothing. Alarmed by its density, I shouted, "To me, lads! Form a tight circle round me to conserve body-heat and prevent anyone getting lost."

"But we are lost, sir," Rubble observed.

Crowhurst started everybody stamping their feet slowly sideways, and cawing like a penguin until I stopped him. The boys enjoyed the novelty of the situation and automatically broke into a kind of chant based on *There's No Place Like Home*. I was reminded of an enormous gramophone record slowly revolving to produce an extremely flat song, and I wondered what would be the reaction of Dr Collins and the boys' parents if they could see us now, lost in a blizzard on Exmoor and groaning round in the penguin survival technique.

At the moment I was experiencing desperate survival problems of a personal nature because I was gradually edged out to the periphery of the circle, where the blast of the north wind took my breath away. Nor could I move back in again, unless I employed unarmed combat. Crowhurst and Rubble seemed to form the central core, and here the disciplined movement of the penguins broke down, because they did not appear to move outwards again. I wondered if emperor penguins who stayed too long on the outside facing the South Pole ever died of frozen kidneys.

Another thing I noticed was that our circular motion seemed to be boring a hole in Exmoor like a huge drill. Already it was difficult to see over the top on the windward side where the snow was piling up in a considerable drift. I heard Crowhurst say, "It's quite warm in the middle, sir. If it's true that the human body generates one kilowatt of heat, we're producing forty kilowatts all together".

"Just you come out here and fe l how much heat I'm generating," I cried bitterly. "Even my tears are solidifying." I refrained from adding that I was experiencing a morbid fear of being entombed, then dug up later by scientists in a perfect state of preservation, like the Siberian mammoths.

"I reckon the drift is high enough for us to build a snow shelter now, sir," Crowhurst declared, "like they teach pilots to do in the RAF on survival training."

I had no idea what he was talking about, but the mere mention of shelter had my whole-hearted support.

"We scoop out a kind of little cave under the drift, sir, making a ledge at the bottom to sleep on. Then our body heat causes condensation on the ceiling, which freezes over and makes everything snug and tight, sir."

"I didn't realize you were ex-RAF, Crowhurst."

"I'm not, sir, but I'm in the cadets."

"Is there anything you're not in?"

"I'm not intoxicated, sir-ha, ha, ha, ha! Not intoxicated, see, sir?"

The boys set to work with a will to construct the survival shelter, glad to have something to do and excited by the novelty of the situation. There was general agreement that directly the job was completed they would eat their emergency rations from the haversacks. They were already on emergency rations because the keen air and exercise had compelled them to eat the packed lunches at nine-thirty in the morning, followed by tea at the new time of noon. As a consequence, supper had been moved forward to half-past one in the afternoon, so that now at only four o'clock they were already eating their emergency rations, washed down with snow. As the boys wolfed down the chocolate, cheese and biscuits, I understood why the danger of cannibalism is still present in the human race. I imagined the Headmaster informing little Spencer Faraday's parents that their son had met with an accident on Exmoor, having been eaten after lights out by his friends, on the Greater Love Hath No Man principle. It occurred to me that if this lot were to climb Everest they would run out of food supplies on the outskirts of Calcutta docks.

I was careful to conceal my own rations in my haversack against the possibility of my having to make a mercy dash for help, but as I sat frozen and depressed in our crude shelter, struggling to think of the right move in such a predicament, Crowhurst produced his Kodak Instamatic. Although I could hardly believe my eyes, he announced he intended to take some holiday snapshots of us for his project, and would we please smile—rather like rounding up the passengers of the *Titanic* for pictures just before she foundered. He also made the important announcement that there was a colour film in the camera ensuring a true record of our unnaturally red noses and blue hands. I sat there in the group with all the vivacity of a corpse, despite his plea for a smile, still bemused by Crowhurst's morbid wish to photograph us perishing in a blizzard. Even as he stood exposed in order to film us, he was rapidly turning into a kind of snowman holding a white camera.

"Now I want Fred to take one of me with sir," Crowhurst said, apparently under the impression we were sunbathing at Bournemouth. "Then I'll take a trick one of Fred buried in the snow, so it looks as if he's only got a head."

My patience exploded. "For pity's sake, boy, you'll soon be able to take a group photo of us all buried in the snow without heads!—sorry, Crowhurst, but I don't think you realize the danger we're in. This is a pretty grim blizzard."

Crowhurst grinned cheerfully. "The worst since 1887, sir, and plenty more coming down from the north. The Pennines are completely blocked, sir, and many Welsh mining villages are cut off."

"How do you know all this?"

"It's on the radio, sir."

"But we haven't got a radio."

Crowhurst indicated a tiny white button in his left ear and a slight bulge in his anorak. "My little transistor, sir."

"Good heavens, lad, and here was I thinking you were wearing a hearing-aid!"

"It is a hearing-aid, sir—else how could I hear the announcer in Bristol?—ha, ha, ha, ha!"

"Let me know if he tells you any good news for a change— like a heat wave coming in from Iceland."

"I'm waiting to see if they say we're missing, sir. Not missing our supper but missing lost, sir—ha, ha, ha, ha!"

As Crowhurst's high-pitched cackle echoed round our new home, I decided I must go back alone for assistance while there was still a chance of getting through. The boys seemed quite cheerful, employing youthful enthusiasm and ingenuity to improve the shelter, as though preparing for years of exile on the moor, tamping down the snow and enlarging the inside cavity as they sang our theme song of *There's No Place Like Home*. But what would the dark fireless night bring, without food or hot drink? I confided my plan to Crowhurst, who insisted I should not worry about the boys, making me feel guilty that my chief worry should be about myself.

I stepped clear of our survival shelter, and, being well over six feet tall, I found that the snow only came up to my shoulders. Taking one pace forward towards civilization and rescue I went down another foot, so that it was necessary to stand on tiptoe to address Crowhurst, who was aiming his camera at me.

"Don't move, sir, I want to snap you like that, with just your head showing above the snow. Say cheese, sir, for the big smile. Coo, this'll look good in my project!—'Mr Pook setting off on a mercy dash'. You are brave, sir, tunnelling through like that."

"Have you no sense of proportion, Crowhurst?" I shouted angrily. "Do you want a photograph of me dying in this white world of silence? Are you so obsessed with that damned project that nothing less will satisfy you but a coloured slide of my clutching hands protruding above the snow?"

"But it's part of my Duke of Edinburgh's Award Scheme, sir. I've already got the bronze, so now I'm trying for the silver. Mr Whittle says I'm one of the youngest boys ever to. . . . "

"Hell's bells, lad, before you fetch it for my inspection can't you see I'm practically buried alive out here and desperately in need of help!"

"I thought you were going to fetch help, sir."

"What I need right now is help to get out of this cursed ravine I'm sinking into."

"I wondered why you chose that side where the ditch is, sir. The flat ground is the other side. . . ."

"Get the lads to pull me out, idiot!"

"But we can't reach you, sir."

"Ye gods, man, use the straps from the haversacks!"

I prayed that no diversion would occur—such as the football results on the radio—to cause the boys to forget me forever while they knotted the straps together and argued if it would not be better to use the brass buckles instead. With juvenile oblivion to peril they were testing their handiwork by arranging a tug-of-war, and I could hear Rubble quarrelling about unequal teams, and little Faraday's shrill voice insisting he pull on the same side as his friend Michael. I shrieked to them in terror to abandon Sports Day and rescue me while they could still locate the crown of my Polar hat.

I heard Crowhurst cry, "Crikey, he's disappeared!" then Rubble said, "P'raps 'e sort of got fed up waitin' like."

For one ghastly moment I feared they would abandon me with youthful indifference in order to continue snowballing each other. Waving my hat to throw off the new layer of snow on it,

I screamed, "Here I am, boys, here I am!" until they cast the lifeline to me.

"Gosh, sir, we nearly lost you in tne gully," Crowhurst informed me as I lay panting and trembling in the comparative security of the shelter. "Now say cheese, sir, while I snap you resting after your ordeal."

I remember my eyes rolling wildly as I automatically bared my teeth for the camera-eyes which had so recently stared death in the face—but I was beyond protesting any more, and quite incapable of speech. Some years before in Ireland a kindly farmer had pointed out a short cut back to civilization across a valley, with the result that within the hour I was fighting for my life in a peat bog and calling upon St Patrick to guide me to firm ground before I disappeared from the face of the earth as a pattern of bubbles. On that occasion I had been taken to hospital for observation and debogging, but today I had to lie there in shock while my body was recorded for the Duke of Edinburgh's future inspection. Moreover, I was required to hear once more Crowhurst's familiar precept that a crashed fighter pilot is immediately sent up in another plane lest he lose his nerve.

"If you leave on the other side of the shelter, sir, you'll be on level ground," Crowhurst advised, depriving me of any excuse to cease being a leader of men, and teaching me never again to appoint him as my deputy during my absence. Crowhurst's lust for power was such that he literally pushed me out of the shelter on the far side, where I sank only up to my knees, reassuring me with the news that "It's barely eight miles back to base, sir, and you can't miss the way because that's how we got here in the first place."

I plodded off in the snow, following Crowhurst's inexplicable advice to pursue the parallel of latitude 51 degrees, 7 minutes, as though it was a motorway, until I reached longitude 3 degrees, 29 minutes, when I must turn north, delivered in a tone implying that I could not miss the line of longitude without tripping over it. My spirits rose because the snow had stopped for several minutes, the route lay mostly downhill and the north wind paralysing my left cheek told me I was on course. In fact, I even began to sing *There's No Place Like Home as* I marched across the moor with that peculiar knees-up step essential to gaining ground in snow. At last I could have a cigarette without being branded as Twentieth Century Man destroying himself and his environment, I thought as I opened the soggy mess that had once been a packet of twenty. But the tobacco tin was watertight, as was indeed my snuff box, so I managed to get the pipe going after I had laboriously dried my lighter. However, the zigzag and semicircular plot of my tracks in the snow warned me not to smoke on the march, caused by the unaccustomed nicotine hitting my head in the pure air with a violence I had not previously experienced since a dentist once gave me a shot of thiopentone, under the delusion that I was chasing his wife when not suffering from toothache. Consequently, I found it expedient to enjoy my pipe whilst lying spread-eagled on the ground.

My watch indicated five-thirty when the snow recommenced, not pretty Christmas-card snow but a real white-out, as though I had fallen into a bakery where there had just been an explosion. I searched desperately for any kind of shelter, unable to recall if an emperor penguin had developed a secondary survival technique when caught alone in a blizzard far from the main flock of rotating relatives. All I could locate was a rock, not exactly the giant Kaaba of Arabia, but about the size of two household dustbins. Although grateful for anything, I discovered empirically that this rock possessed two unusual features. Firstly, it appeared to have no lee side, so that wherever I crouched the blizzard blew into me. Secondly, it manifested what I may call an aural mirage; whereby when I put my ear to it I could hear the sea, like listening to a conch shell. I wondered if fate had led me to the only rock in the world which built up a snowdrift on every side of it, and then hypnotized its victim with the sound of waves breaking on a distant shore.

I hollowed out a little survival shelter as best I could, although at times I felt that I was struggling to save the rock from being buried rather than myself. It was necessary to bale out fresh snow from the shelter every few minutes, like a leaking boat, but at least I had this musical rock to crouch against. Obviously the next task was to check my position with map and compass, though how to do this without radar I had little idea. From the haversack I extracted the map, thinking it odd that our official large-scale map should have Princetown marked on it, not to mention Dartmoor prison, and managed to squeeze in Plymouth on the border. Puzzled, I turned to the map title and discovered it was a map of Dartmoor. On the reverse side was Cornwall, and a detailed inset of the Scilly Isles.

Fortunately I had been issued with a school compass in a perspex case, but upon lining it up I noticed that the blue north arm of the pointer had broken off from the central brass pivot and lay useless on the dial marking the cardinal points.

But at least I had bandages, five altogether. I knew I had bandages when I opened the cellophane package containing my emergency rations—and what I needed most right now was food, not bandages. At first I thought it must be the normal administrative error common to all expeditions, whereby men have been sent into the Malay jungle bearing skis, and up Everest equipped with shark repellent. Back in the Royal Marines, I myself was put ashore at Jaffa loaded down with a crate of oranges issued by the Quartermaster at Deal Barracks.

At first I wondered if I was lost in a blizzard on Exmoor with a broken compass, five bandages and a map of Dartmoor as a result of Crowhurst's paranoia, but then I remembered that it was Rent-a-Beast himself who had packed and issued the rucksacks—"Just as an airman relies on his parachute, so your life may depend on your rucksack," he had said, handing me the equipment. I figured that had I been an airman I should now be a mere hole in the earth's crust. Rent-a-Beast was my code name for Whittle ever since he had referred to my red nose as Dunkery Beacon; a poor jest because it was no longer red but blue.

I prayed for the snow to cease feathering down so I could see where I was, and eventually it did and I saw where I was, so that I closed my eyes in disbelief. My rock was no ordinary rock but a boulder, and no ordinary boulder but an overhanging one, overhanging some two hundred feet of cliff. I discovered it was located on a tiny promontory of cliff-top, so that when I had walked round it earlier in search of the lee side I had been virtually walking in space. Not only could I hear the sea now but I could plainly perceive it far below, breaking on the whitened rocks.

But at least I knew where I was— on the north coast of Somerset—and when I stepped cautiously from my shelter, trying to tiptoe away from the north coast of Somerset, I knew where I was going—heading for the Bristol Channel feet first.

It was a terrifying experience in a silent world of non-friction, where everything one grasped simply crumbled or was coated with rime, so that one descended painlessly and swiftly, like grain from an elevator, the silence broken only by my shrieks of horror. Because Somerset had run out of land at this point I was dumped straight into the sea, discovering by experiment that it was about nine feet deep and less cold than the river—that is to say free of icebergs.

No cries of terror now, but the silent resolution of a man fighting to draw breath in tiny gasps with the mouth at maximum aperture, like an eagle chick waiting for mother to return with dinner. Surely the Fates were not so efficient that directly one had an evil thought about Rent-a-Beast one was ejected two hundred feet into the sea and drowned?

There was no foothold for me at the base of the cliff, but

there was a rock offshore shaped like an old wisdom-tooth, which I determined to gain. I have always been a powerful swimmer, especially in an ocean, so, mustering all my strength for the ordeal ahead, I struck out in the hope I could cover the distance of some six yards before I went down exhausted.

I collapsed on the rock in considerable distress, glad only that Crowhurst was not present with his camera to record such extreme prostration for his project. You will appreciate my condition if I tell you that it was necessary to compose myself for a full minute before the gradual accumulation of reserve strength enabled me to swivel my eyeballs slightly to one side in order to observe the gull which had landed on the rock to check if lunch had arrived unexpectedly. Those graceful white birds which enliven the seaside appear deceptively small until one is perched on your backside, under the impression you have been washed up as edible flotsam. This gull was fit, alert and bursting with food, about the size of a small swan, and equipped with a beak like a pickaxe obviously the British equivalent of the African vulture, only larger. So large, in fact, that for a moment I expected to be carried off in his talons. A wave broke over the rock and the wash rolled my torso sufficiently to send him off.

And so it was at the seaside on the third day of my Easter holidays that I perished amid the beautiful scenery of our national heritage, only six yards from my native land—yet another victim of man's age-old blunder of listening to women.

EIGHT

From a distance it appeared that Mrs Tassington-Lee had succeeded in domesticating the common house-mop, but closer inspection revealed that the mop was fitted with a castor at each corner, enabling it to move across the beach emitting a yapping kind of squeak. Furthermore, Mrs Tassington-Lee addressed the mop as Rebel, or to be more precise, Heel, Rebel, heel, whereupon the mop paused long enough to raise one castor and water the heel of the lady's shoe, then glide off once again over the sandy shore.

It is well-known that one end of a chihuahua is fitted with a nose, though which end is difficult to ascertain until it raises that organ to sniff, and the lady's neighbours hinted that she had taken to exercising one of her house mice on a lead. Nevertheless, it was Rebel who located the body lying on the sand at the foot of a high rock, and he was extremely excited about the find because it was his first success with bodies larger than a sea squirt.

Mrs Tassington-Lee, clad in tweeds against the onslaught of the English summer, arrived at the scene with trepidation. "Heel, Rebel, heel," she commanded anxiously, whereupon Rebel left the body only long enough to moisten her shoe like a canine water-pistol before returning to his triumph. His next duty was to copyright the body by establishing his claim in the fashion of dogs the world over, with a lightning baptism ceremony on the head and feet, followed by the territorial warning halfway along the border.

The body moaned the word "Hel' " twice, because I had not sufficient strength to make the lip explosion involved in the letter P.

Mrs Tassington-Lee knelt beside me in deep concern. "Oh you poor man, there must have been a shipwreck! Shall I phone the lifeboat station at Minehead?"

"Not shipwrecked. Fell over cliff, then fell off rock. Hel'."

Falling off the rock had been a most extraordinary business. I came to or woke up at dawn, when some primeval survival urge caused me to throw myself into the sea in order to swim back to the cliff. But in some remarkable way the sea had departed, so that I lay stunned on the sand, gazing up at the rock and wondering if the Bristol Channel had dried up during the night, like the Red Sea in the Bible. This impression was strengthened when I found there was no trace of the sea anywhere. The cliff was still there, but to the north was a desert of sand, as though one could walk across to Barry Island and South Wales, visible on the horizon.

"Sea gone," I moaned. Surely this was not a nightmare from which I had awakened and jumped out of my bedroom window?

The lady felt my forehead. "It's low tide—low tide, when the sea goes out," she explained, as if I was a rustic who had never been to the seaside. "At this time of year we have abnormally low tides, then the sea comes in again and that's high tide. You see, that is why there's no snow on the beach and Rebel can have walkies. He can't move in snow because he's so tiny."

"What time high tide?" I asked urgently. If Rebel couldn't cope with snow his chances would be pretty thin in a twelve-foot tide—even less than mine.

"Oh, it's barely on the turn. Can you possibly walk back?"

"Can't stand up." I tried to draw her attention to the sand crater I was lying in as a result of throwing myself off the rock and breaking every bone in my body, hitting the beach like a human meteorite. Mrs Tassington-Lee seemed to think I had tripped over a pebble. Only Rebel realized the gravity of the situation, regarding himself as a giant St Bernard rescue mastiff locating me on the Alps and trying to revive me with his water-pistol.

"You stay here while I fetch assistance," Mrs Tassington-

Lee advised me, lest I should accompany her on the mission. "Heel, Rebel!"

Rebel dutifully moistened his mistress's shoe, then, putting his tiny legs into top gear, followed her along the beach with a blur of paws. I lay there hoping she would return before the tide did, and wondering what the Duke of Edinburgh would say if I was carried into Buckingham Palace so he could see what lengths his Awards drive men to.

They laid me to rest in the sick-bay of Butlin's Holiday Camp at Minehead, where two thousand children were being entertained in a pre-season Activity Week. A triumphantly smug Mr Whittle informed me how my party had been rescued only half an hour after I had deserted them, and that my little escapade smacked of a suicide attempt on my part following my failure as a leader of men.

I lay prostrate, unable to defend my reputation or even reply. The visiting medico, Dr Jackson, advised me I was suffering from shock, exposure and severe bruising, but seemed unable to grasp that I was slowly passing away in front of his very eyes, informing me that I could get up as soon as I liked because the bed was needed for a patient.

In the next bed was Stephen Squires, victim of a Tarzan-like leap from tree to tree, but had suffered the misfortune to land on the branch upon his genitals, with the result that Crowhurst had dubbed him Taurus the Bull and suggested he would have to walk about with a wheelbarrow for the remainder of the holiday. The boys showed commendable sympathy for their wounded comrade, visiting him in relays to inspect his remarkable condition, but Miss Dewar had to talk privately to the girls in order to put Stephen out of bounds as far as they were concerned.

Mr Whittle tucked a typed sheet of foolscap under my cheek, so I could read it with my left eye. "This is tomorrow's Activity Programme, Pook. I am down for Roller-skating, Miss Dewar will take the girls for Swimming. As you still seem somewhat under the weather I have allocated you an indoor activity—Mixed Judo."

"Mix' Ju'!"

"Yes, Mixed Judo. I've been compelled to postpone the Boys' Karate until you are fully recovered—say the following day."

"Ill. So ill."

"Oh, stop play-acting, Pook. All right, so you've got a bruise or two, but in a situation like this you can't expect to opt out of your responsibilities and throw the whole weight upon Miss Dewar and me. Next to you is Stephen Squires with a dramatically swollen doodah, causing him to walk like a tripod. Next to him is Mark Roper with galloping asthma. Eleven children have broken out in rashes as big as streaky bacon. Fiona Lovejoy has been rushed to Taunton Hospital with appendicitis. Belinda Sprockett is homesick and has threatened to end it all with a bottle of aspirins. Michael Gunter has developed spots in places where normal children don't even have places. Theresa Shrubb still has her earring lodged inside her ear—for heaven's sake don't ask me why. Fred Rubble has lost his chalet key and claims to have swallowed it. Angela Bates is having morning sickness night and day."

"Nothing untoward then."

"Nothing untoward if we were back at school—but we're supposed to be on an adventure holiday."

"Sounds like we've succeeded."

"Worst of all, Brenda Shannon has fallen in love again and is having fits. There's a lad on the camp from a remand school—so tough that the teachers have to outnumber the pupils, even at church service. This Roderick is a Skinhead with big ears and no eyebrows; tall and thin, like a banana with bovver boots, and extremely short braces to hold his jeans up under the armpits. So of course it was love at first sight for

Brenda when she saw her knight in shining denim, and they embraced to exchange colds."

"I thought she was engaged to a Greaser?"

"A girl can't wait for ever—that was a week ago. Now she's having night fits, and I hold her down while she shakes. Once she's got the rhythm she starts moaning 'Rod-derrick! Rod-derrick!' in time with the fit, like a football chant. It is extremely harrowing, so I expect you to take over tonight."

"I suppose tonight she'll be chanting 'Muhammed Rassani! Muhammed Rassani!' — you know how fickle she is."

Our boys, biologically younger than the girls, were much more interested in sport than in courtship. But for the girls the chase was on with instinctive prowess. Each evening their slacks and sweaters were discarded in favour of battle dresses and tights, reinforced with the armour of jewellery and war paint. Most of them looked like beautiful angels in the perfection of teenage, except for the huge platform shoes decreed by fashion, so large for their slender legs as to render them slightly club-footed. One or two girls overdid the make-up, especially Theresa Shrubb, who appeared to be wearing a death mask, and Angela Bates, whose experiments with eyelashes and eyeliners gave the impression she had just seen a ghost in her chalet and was unable to recover from the shock. I examined Theresa closely in case she had succeeded in fitting blue plastic eyelids into the sockets, and Miss Dewar had a private word with her about letting down the hem of the dress to cover her buttocks more completely when she stood upright.

To guard against the mystery of the lost earring Theresa now wore a kind of gold bangle from each lobe which would be safe on an elephant, and to engage the attention of potential boyfriends there reposed in her handbag a six-inch rubber spider connected to a long metal spring. She was in the habit of dangling this lure on boys' heads from behind, gradually letting the spider creep down the lads' faces, on the assumption that it would induce them to chase her in a frenzy of passion. Rumour had it that this courting ritual had been the cause of the earring becoming lodged in the meatus of her ear.

Equipped by nature with eagle vision whereby they could detect a male at a thousand paces even by moonlight, the girls set out for that paradoxical modern entertainment, the discotheque, where they danced together without boys to the music recorded by their pop idols—a sound which always put me in mind of living next door to an angry neighbour who perpetually shouted abuse at you over the garden wall as he bashed his dustbin. The hall was packed with girls performing the monotonous gyrations of the dance, but scarcely a boy in sight. Conversation was necessarily eliminated by the power of electronic transmission, around eighty decibels in an octave, so when on my duty rounds I employed a simple system of tick-tack to ensure the girls were all right by raising my thumb, to which they replied by smiling and raising theirs. I observed that Belinda Sprockett had postponed her suicide plans in order to bob up and down with her peers, a performance accentuated by two horns of hair dyed a yellowy white to contrast with her dark locks. Also bobbing in unison were her pendant earrings, chunky beads, a 36 bust and her chalet key suspended by a neck string. Pinned to her dress was one of those alarming badges people buy at the seaside informing us that: 'Boy wanted for night work experience preferred.' Brenda Shannon's badge was even more explicit : 'Visit my chalet, boys. Knock twice and ask for mercy.'

Yet despite these displays of bravado the girls were inwardly virginal to the point of primness—contrary to the popular press —preserving themselves with almost sexless modesty against the goal of their lives, the traditional white wedding. It must be difficult for the general public to understand how the permissive society has been wished on these children by the mass media, or to appreciate how that campaign has failed utterly to influence their near Victorian propriety. As Mr Mould so often prayed—dear God, preserve us from sensational journalism and let the public think for itself.

Mr Mould, of course, had a prayer for everything, including the University of the Air, who had solved the age-old problem of discipline at last—teachers without pupils present. The packed hall of girls were now dutifully screaming upon hearing a record by the current superstar, Tiny Tommy Osborne, who symbolized the American aim to abolish childhood entirely by informing us in a nasal yet treble pipe that he had endured the major emotional traumas of life at the early age of ten. It seemed his beloved had not been terrew to him, leaving him a broken wreck by deserting him for an old roué of twelve, so that the whole world laughed at his grief. Ahead of him lay nothing but the lonely twilight of adolescence, with only memories of his fickle baby to haunt him as he dozed by the fireside, a wrinkled old teenager.

Because the disco closed at 9.30 the girls had one whole glorious hour of freedom till curfew. The majority returned to the chalets to collapse on their beds in fatigue. Most of the boys were already unconscious, exhausted by the day's activities and anaesthetized by that mild chloroform called Somerset air. Insensible to the point where we were able to carry the body of Michael Gunter, partly upside-down, from a friend's chalet to his own without waking him. Some of the children could not be roused by shouts, pushes or cold water—I managed to wake Laura Lovell only by pinching her ear with my fingernails for several minutes, and even then she came to in easy stages and relapsed into slumber directly I left her. Fred Rubble rolled out of his bed most nights without waking, to pass the small hours crumpled on the floor as though he had lately fallen from a steeple, as near death as a healthy boy can be. Thus it was impossible to gain admittance to most chalets by knocking or shouting, unless one possessed a master key. Walking my night rounds of duty reminded me of exploring the ancient catacombs beneath Rome, surrounded by bodies who slept for ever.

But the jet set, the night people, who preferred to live dangerously on the razor's edge hurried to the spacious coffee bar for cokes and jungle courtship—jungle in the sense that having attracted one's quarry one chased it screaming round the house. Little Jackie Fordham demonstrated a more sophisticated approach. Having espied her prey—a hirsute young man with the deadpan face of contemporary romance—she purchased a coke for Crowhurst, who happened to be sitting next to the stranger, then walked over to surprise Crowhurst with such novel generosity. The young man soon experienced Jackie's feminine wiles in the shape of the quivering rubber spider covering his head and walking down his face with unnerving realism.

Now the chase was on amid screams and an arpeggio of feet over the dance floor—so slippery that little Jackie was able to elude her pursuer despite the high multi-coloured shoes encumbering her thin legs. When she decided male pride must be satisfied by letting him catch her, she completed her conquest by offering him the ambrosia of Aphrodite, some warm Smith's Crisps; and to assure him her love was true she battered him to the ground with a cushion from the settee.

"How old are you, Jackie?" I inquired when she returned to the bar to buy her prey a coke to revive him.

"Fifteen, sir."

"Fifteen! What will you be like when you're twenty?"

"Married, sir."

"Do you know that fellow you've just . . . er . . . just been talking to?"

"No, sir, but I do now. I wanted him for my birthday."

"When is your birthday, dear?"

"Today, sir. Aren't I lucky?"

Once again I found myself buying cokes all round as I sat

138

there at the bar like an outsize gooseberry in order to supervise the orgy until the 10.30 round-up of young love. How was it, I asked myself, that whenever I asked the girls their age it was invariably their blessed birthday?

"Thank you very much, sir," Jackie smiled beguilingly as she clattered off on her five-inch platforms bearing a tray of cokes. "Oh really, sir, isn't he lovely? His name's Bill and he comes from Brixton. See you, sir."

I glanced across at Brixton Bill, wondering what was to-day's criterion of loveliness that made Jackie sigh so deeply as she romantically thrust the neck of the coke bottle into his mouth, like a mother force-feeding her infant.

At 10.30 I rounded up our delightful and friendly children without protest, that they might guide me back to our lines in this massive encampment. They knew the way, just as they knew every nook and cranny of the camp already. The others had retired earlier, exhausted by swimming, judo, tennis, roller-skating, fencing, trampolining, football and all the other delights of the holiday complex.

Only Crowhurst had to be ushered inside from the temporary observatory he had set up on the chalet roof—telescope, star almanac, chart and torch—to study the heavens whilst lesser men slumbered. Later on, after midnight, I saw on my rounds a telescope protruding from the transom window of a darkened chalet, and heard a muted voice saying, "Canis Major, Rigel, Betelgeux, Procyon, Sirius, Alphard, Eridanus, Cetus, Orion, Taurus, Aldebaran, Pleiades, Gemini, Castor, Pollux, Auriga, Capella. . . ."

When next I passed the chalet the monotonous drone was still emerging. "Spica, Virgo, Regulus, Leo, Arcturus, Bootes, Ursa Major, Hercules, Draco, Polaris, Cepheus, Vega, Cassiopeia. . . ."

Surely he didn't intend doing the whole universe, I thought to myself. I called softly, "That's all for tonight, Crowhurst."

The voice said, "Oh no, sir, the earth continues to rotate, you know. It doesn't stop during the night. I'm trying to cover as much sky as possible before the moon comes up and blots them out."

"What time does the moon rise tonight?"

"4.13257 by Atomic Time, sir."

"What time is that on my primitive hour-glass type clockwork watch?"

"Just after 4 a.m., sir. Atomic Time is based on the radiations which caesium atoms emit, and is far more accurate than sidereal. . . ."

"I'm dog tired, Crowhurst."

"The radio time signal used to go six pips, sir, but now it goes pip, pip, pip, pip, pip, peep. That last peep is Atomic Time, sir. Now, about the moon, sir. . . ."

"When are you being transferred to Grammar School, Crowhurst?"

"I don't want to go, sir. My Dad says I'm just as well off at the top of a Secondary School."

"But you'd be happier at the top of a Grammar School."

"No, sir. My Dad says where else would I have a real live author like you to teach me English. That's why I'm writing a novel for my English project, sir. I'm on page 200 already."

"Practically finished the first chapter, I suppose? Anyhow, go to bed now, lad, before you wake your room-mates."

Crowhurst chuckled. "They wouldn't wake up if a meteorite hit the chalet, sir. Still, I know it's rather late, so night-night, sir. Sweet dreams about Miss Dewar, sir—ha, ha, ha, ha!"

"Good-night, Crowhurst."

I sauntered off to check on the girls' chalets, but at the corner of the block I turned and waited in the shadows. Down the lines I could distinguish a long black object emerge from a transom window and point itself towards Jupiter, but I ignored it and moved on.

140

Girls are strange creatures. From the first chalet came a familiar rhythmic voice like a psychic message being relayed by a medium. It gasped, "Sid-den-ney! . . . Sid-den-ney! . . . Sid-den-ney! . . ." so I deduced it was Brenda Shannon's new mating call to replace Roderick. I mused what the effect would be if she fell for an Indian boy named Mustapha Curry.

From my vantage point in the darkness I watched a door open, to reveal Michele Bassett's head, her hair secured by two elastic bands. Having checked both ways to see if the coast was clear she stepped out, clad only in a pink nightie. Her artless strategy of switching on the light before looking out enabled me to see the youthful beauty of her face and figure as though she were floodlit on a stage. Her hair shone like copper around the white column of her neck, so that she might have been an angel visiting the children in some old fairy tale.

I watched fascinatedly, wondering what midnight tryst she had planned—this graceful Juliet in a nylon gown who glided noiselessly to the adjacent chalet on dainty toes. I was soon to learn.

Banging heavily on the door of Brenda's chalet she shrieked, "For God's sake shut your face, you old bat! Any more Sid-den-ney out of you and I'll fetch Mr Pook to lance your boil."

I shrank back into the shadows, disillusioned and appalled by the boil threat. Miss Dewar had told me how Brenda had a boil which would preclude further horse-riding unless she adopted the crouch position of jockeys on the final furlong. Just as I remembered that Michele was on migraine tablets, a haggard Mr Whittle accosted me holding the first-aid bag in one hand and the biggest bunch of keys I had ever seen in the other; the two-foot bunch necessary for opening every chalet in the block.

"Panic stations, Pook!" he cried, yet softly so that only he and I would run berserk in the silent night.

"Crowhurst can't get the telescope out of his eye?"

"Don't joke, man, it may cost us our jobs. Because we live

in the land of the dead as far as our kids are concerned, I've had to obtain this bunch of duplicate keys from the office. First, we'll have to open every chalet to check."

"To see if they're asleep?"

"Be kind to me, Pook. I've already been round like Dr Finley's Casebook, treating everything from blisters to beriberi —sometimes I think the Duke of Edinburgh's Award qualifies one for the Royal College of Surgeons—and now, at two o'clock in the morning, we're a girl short. Understand, Pook? —a sixteen-year-old female is missing!"

"Well, at least she's over the age of consent."

Whittle clenched his fists to his forehead. "I'm begging you not to bring sex into this, Pook, just to make it worse. Maybe she couldn't sleep and decided to go for a walk, eh?"

"Maybe she could sleep and decided to go for a sleepwalk?"

"That's it, Pook, that's it! You've got it—somnambulism."

"Maybe she sleep-walked round to her boyfriend's chalet, and now she's sleeping with him."

"Shut up, Pook! Don't say another word. Let me do the talking. Stephanie Anderson woke up and discovered Susan Cooper wasn't in Sheila Slade's bed, so she reported it to me."

"What was she doing in Sheila's bed anyway?"

"Prepare yourself for Peyton Place. It seems that Roma Long has been two-timing with Susan's boyfriend, so they broke friends and Susan quit her chalet for Stephanie's—at midnight if you please—and shared Sheila's bed. Then Stephanie woke up just now and noticed she had gone."

"Where is Sheila?"

"Sheila knows nothing about this business. She is still in the bed in the deep coma our kids enter instead of slumber. She wouldn't know the difference if we took the bed away to the police station. Anyhow, before we phone the police we must search every chalet."

We commenced our hunt through the catacombs at 2.30,

switching on the lights and checking each corpse against the roster sheet. Every boy had passed away in his bed, except Fred Rubble, who lay crumpled on the floor as if the victim of a hit-and-run driver. Only chalet 243 displayed any form of life, where I discovered Crowhurst fully dressed under the blankets, nursing his telescope and pretending to be asleep. I pulled the quilt down to cover his boots so his feet would not get cold, then moved on.

We were unable to obtain the services of Miss Dewar to check the girls' chalets because she had flipped the safety-catch on her door, rendering the duplicate key inoperative. Shouts and bangs were ineffectual, for it seemed that to wake people who had been knocked out by the local ozone one had to force an entry and employ physical violence on their person.

Mr Whittle and I systematically checked every chalet for the missing girl, unheeded by the occupants, who lay in every posture of unconsciousness as though the camp had undergone a gas attack. I noticed, but did not comment on, Whittle's nervous inspection of cupboards, under beds—and even in small trinket drawers, as though he half suspected that Susan Cooper had been dismembered by the girls and packed neatly away in glove drawers.

"That does it, Pook," Whittle hissed when we had drawn a blank right along the lines. "Back to square one and question the two girls at the scene of the crime."

This was easier said than done because Stephanie Anderson who had made the original report was now asleep. She occupied the top bunk bed, and in his endeavours to wake her by sitting her up Mr Whittle seemed unable to prevent her falling forward over his shoulder like a rag doll, so that he stood there apparently demonstrating the fireman's lift.

Meanwhile I had got our other key witness, Sheila Slade, into a sitting position, where she lay in my arms with her head so far back that I feared her neck was broken. I addressed the underside of her chin without success, then shouted up her nostrils to wake up, again to no avail.

"Perry Mason never had it so tough as this," I commented, to account for Whittle losing his temper and shaking Stephanie all over the bed. He was definitely losing his nerve too, shouting "Wake up, you dozy mare, wake up! First you ruin my career, then when I want to interrogate, you die on me!"

"Try Sheila for a change," I suggested. "She's the one who let Susan share her bed."

Sheila did not fulfil the conventional role of a key witness. She was hanging out of bed with her head upside-down, yet breathing deeply and loudly, her face expressionless and oblivious to her responsibilities.

"I'll try slapping her face," Whittle said.

"Mind you don't break her jaw then. . . ." Just as I delivered the warning Sheila slid out of bed quite slowly, and now lay prostrate on the carpet in her red nightdress, breathing almost to a snore.

"How in hell do they ever wake up for breakfast?" Whittle groaned.

"That's odd—Sheila's left the bed, yet there's still a lump there," I observed.

Whittle threw back the blankets, to reveal a curled-up body in a lemon nightdress at the foot of the bed. "Merciful heaven, it's Susan Cooper!" he shouted, like an unsuccessful conjurer.

"Is she asphyxiated?"

"Even worse—she's asleep."

We knew she was asleep by the heaving of her bosom—an unmistakable sign with Susan because the other girls alleged she had worn a bra since she was six. Roma Long even hinted that as a toddler Susan often overbalanced and fell forward on her face for the same reason.

"You see what happened, Pook," Whittle explained, now Sherlock Holmes running his hand across the mattress. "The double weight caused the spring to sag, whereupon Susan gradually slipped down the bed. That's why we missed her when we counted heads."

"Next time we'd better count something else and divide by two."

"Now let's repark the bodies and get some sleep ourselves."

Hard to believe unless you have had a similar experience with children, but we put Stephanie and Sheila to bed, then carried Susan back to her own chalet—all without breaking their slumber.

"Delightful kids really," I remarked, as the camp clock registered three.

"Yes, Pook, they're pretty good by and large. It's the staff who get me down."

"Well, I'm not just a straw in the wind. I don't care what the others say about you—I like you. Good-night."

When this unique holiday closed we sat in the coach pleasantly exhausted in mind and body, each with his own memories. The pupils had been shopping for presents to surprise the family, particularly Mum, and they had returned laden with the handiwork of Hong Kong and Japan—a nightmare concave mirror for the parlour which flashed when you looked into it, a lampshade which chimed when switched on, ashtrays in the shape of lavatory pans, sewing boxes designed for midgets, giant oscillating scorpions to hang in the bathroom, and a hideous backscratcher employing Dracula's fangs for the job.

Only Roy Plack relished our departure with the immortal words, "I misses me telly." Everybody else would have stayed on if possible, but as that was out of the question they requested a return next year. With last minute waves and kisses we drove away, and as we headed east I heard a familiar voice behind me moaning, "Wolfgang! Wolfgang! Wolfgang! . . ."

145

Looking round puzzledly I discovered it to be a weeping Brenda Shannon, well equipped with tissues for the journey, waving through the rear window to a speck on the horizon.

"Must be the new Common Mark t spirit," I remarked to Miss Dewar as we settled down for the long ride home.

NINE

Meanwhile, back at the ranch, everything was normal. Miss Wright, one of our P.E. mistresses, had a black eye as the result of a left hook from a militant Mum. Militant Mums came up to the school bent on rough justice, their cases resting on the shaky evidence of their offspring, who naturally enough blamed the school for everything. The school was particularly prone to lose the pupils' coats, pens and even to steal their money. Just as the school could not differentiate between right and wrong, detaining innocent children after lessons.

Right now our child saint, Linda Bracket, was explaining to Dr Collins how she had not told her mother the real truth about the shower. Miss Wright had not forced Linda to have a shower after Games despite Linda being a martyr to colds. Linda was not a martyr to colds, it seemed, but had not wanted to shower because she had lost her towel. Miss Wright was nursing a black eye and Linda cried now, not out of sympathy for Miss Wright but because she guessed she too would soon have one.

Linda's militant Mum marched her off, and when I looked down the drive from the office window I discovered how right she was. I did not often feel sorry for Linda but this was one occasion when I did.

We also had one or two indignant Dads on our books, who wrote us typed letters couched in the stern phraseology of the law, full of 'My son has brought it to my notice', and 'I expect the school to make full financial restitution in respect of my son's shorts which disappeared during the course of the school outing arranged by you and during which time he was legally under your jurisdiction as in *loco parentis*'.

To answer such letters we always interviewed the aggrieved pupil and sent his dad a verbatim report of the conversation, usually like this:

"Where did you lose your shorts, Stephen?"

"I dunno, sir."

"Well, where did you go?"

"We went on the beach to swim, then on the pier, then on the funfair, then in the caff, then on the donkeys, then up the cliffs, then on the canoes, then in the swimming-pool, then. . . ."

"Do you remember what time you missed the shorts, Stephen?"

"Eight o'clock, sir, when I come home."

"Did you report the loss to any of the teachers?"

"No, sir."

"Why not?"

"I dunno, sir. I forgot."

"Have you asked the other two hundred children on the trip if they saw your shorts or took them by mistake?"

"No, sir."

"Have you or your father returned to Brighton and searched the area for your shorts, and phoned the lost property office of Brighton Corporation to see if they have been handed in?"

"No, sir."

"Have you or your father contacted Brighton Police to report your loss?"

"No, sir."

"Thank you, Stephen. Tell your dad we shall be writing to him today."

It was not our intention to embarrass Stephen, but we felt hurt. Despite the massive operation of taking two hundred children to the seaside safely and happily we did not anticipate gratitude, but neither did we relish reprimand for some trivial incident beyond our control. Perhaps too few parents realize what teachers do for the children, often far beyond the requirements of their employment; such as extra tuition, evening games and holiday trips. Certainly that is why many of our pupils regarded school as the centre of their lives and were loath to depart at the bell.

Of course, we had many exemplary parents, but if only more would visit the schools, discover what their children are doing—some of the results are real eye-openers—and let them see their elders take an interest in their work. Sad to reflect that even today some homes are still television-ridden, bookless, talkless places to eat and sleep in. Oh Parents, tell your children the old nursery rhymes and show them the flowers and the sunrise.

"And," said Mr Mould, addressing an almost empty staff room, "We shall not argue with your experts, nor debate with your highbrows, nor defend ourselves against your radicals—but we shall show them the facts of life *in situ*. And we shall say unto them, Come, my friends, argue no more, talk no more, attack no more, but—in the words of Dr Arnold at Rugby School in 1828—put your money where your mouth is and do the job with us."

"I'm sure Dr Arnold never said that, Mr Mould," I suggested.

"I merely put his dictum into modern parlance for your benefit, Pook, so kindly have the courtesy to shut down your curry disposal unit while I am speaking. Misquotation is fashionable today, for it seems our students at Cudford University have translated Voltaire as declaring: 'I disapprove of what you say, but I will defend to the death your right not to say it.'"

"In what context, Mr Mould?"

"Ever zealous for the maintenance of free speech and democracy some fifteen of our brave young men stormed the platform without regard for their personal safety and knocked me to the ground before I could contaminate the audience with my reactionary views concerning education. Despite the odds they managed to overpower me and break my glasses, until I was rescued by some Fascist pigs who do not understand our new freedom and try to thwart our new democracy. I tried to warn them not to help an enemy of the people, but they heeded not and ruthlessly carried me out of the hall to safety. Ah, Pook, the Bible put it best: 'Ye shall know them by their works'. Judge folks not by what they say, but by what they do."

"All the graduates I've met have been excellent fellows, Mr Mould. I reckon we're lucky to have practically no politics in this school."

Mr Mould puffed his pipe. "True, Pook, true. Very few have the strange death-wish to serve foreign masters in order to encompass our own destruction. Personally, I lost interest in politics when Russia abandoned Communism for Imperialism. However, watch Whittle—red as a monkey's fud. Chip on his shoulder as big as that elm tree in the quad because he can't get promotion. Should be issued with chopsticks in the school canteen and wear a pigtail.

"You mean to say Whittle is a Maoist!"

"An unbigoted Maoist."

"Whatever's that, Mr Mould?"

"Well, if there was a Nazi revival, Whittle would become an unbigoted Nazi and teach in a black shirt and jackboots. Listen, Peter, if Whittle had to teach our First Year *Mary Had a Little Lamb* it would sound like this:

> 'Mary had a little lamb,
> Mein Fuhrer shot it dead.
> Now it goes to school with her
> Between two lumps of bread.'

Observe also how his swarthy complexion and shoe-brush moustache mark him as a South American revolutionary—an unsuccessful South American revolutionary; one whom his comrades would bribe to change sides so they could win; one upon whose head the Government would place, not a bounty, but a free pardon."

"The Sydney Carton of education, eh? Well, there goes the bell so I'm off to take the Brain of Britain."

"A delightful collection of scholars, Pook, especially

Crowhurst and Gloria Pyle."

"Strange how the glamour girls so often have the awful names. Her best bet is to marry someone such as Whitlow and change it."

"Like John Darling in the Third Year. Very tough on a boy to go through school with a name like that without fights."

"That is why Hollywood used to rename so many of its actresses. Extremely dffficult to become a screen goddess as Eva Brick, so she had to become Tania Sorrento."

"I feel most sorry for Debra Smelley. Every time she tells you her name it sounds like a confession."

Crowhurst opened the classroom door for me standing to attention, giving the military salute because I had served in the Marines, then the naval salute in respect for my naval service. "Welcome aboard to the best teacher in the school, sir," he said, with what he imagined to be an engaging smile. "I have already distributed the 116 books required by the class for this lesson, sir, and I have also taken the liberty to clean the board, open the windows and distribute 38 rulers."

"No rose on my desk?"

"Only a Toffo and my homework, sir. Please don't forget to set the class homework, sir, and masses of extra homework for me. My dad does the homework too, sir, and when he's finished we compare notes."

"Who marks his then?"

"I have taken the liberty of enclosing dad's in my own folder, sir. He says he can't miss the opportunity of being taught English by a famous author, sir."

"How about your mum?"

"She's pregnant, sir."

I spent so many evenings not only marking Crowhurst's extra studies but also finding more work to set him that I did not relish his dad adding to the load. I had been secretly toying with the idea of setting him a monster English project in five stages, each stage of which I would reveal to him on the completion of the previous one, similar to the Labours of Hercules, which would last him till one of us left the school. Section one would require him to read the entire Forsyte S ga, whereupon it would be necessary for him to summarize the books in his folder. Stage three would involve his reading either the complete works of Dickens or The Oxford Shakespeare, then summarize as before. Lastly I would give him a written assignment, thus: 'Compare the Forsyte Saga with Tolstoy's *War and Peace,* then do the same with Tolstoy's *Anna Karenina'.*

So Crowhurst would say, "But, sir, I haven't done Tolstoy." Now I could play my trump card. "Sorry about that, Crowhurst; my mistake. I should have said Tolstoy, not Dickens. Get your reading glasses on and make up for lost time, lad."

On my desk reposed his answers to my question sheet on *Ivanhoe,* which I selected not so much for its literary merit as its bulk—500 pages—and small print. Even Crowhurst could not devour *Ivanhoe* in a single night, and at the other extreme Debra Smelley, the human snail, took three years to read *Jane Eyre.*

As in all my question sheets for Crowhurst and family, the final question was what I termed the land-mine—so that if you managed to answer the previous nineteen, number twenty blew you to pieces. Question twenty was so contrived that few scholars in the land could answer it at all, and only Sir Walter Scott himself could know the full solution.

Held in reserve up my sleeve was the Oxford Chaucer, which I intended to drop on Crowhurst when at his lowest ebb, such as during the next flu epidemic, because not only did it contain 717 pages in double columns like the Bible, but also there were a further 149 pages of Middle English vocabulary to be learned before you could understand the previous 717 pages of text. I had been gradually preparing the ground for Chaucer by impressing upon Crowhurst that the true student of our language could no more overlook Chaucer than he could Shakespeare.

I figured that once I got Crowhurst in bed with flu, then presented him with a work vital to the development of English literature which he could not understand, I would have gained the upper hand at last. If all else failed I was resolved to go the whole hog by returning to 700 A.D. and give him *Beowulf* on a parchment scroll.

"Please sir, I ain't got no pen," Gloria informed me in Modern English. "Can I lend yours?"

"Lend it to whom, Gloria?"

"I mean borry it, sir."

How, I asked myself, did the pupils manage to preserve our ancient patois in the teeth of my endless barrage of exercises, verbal instruction and perusal of the classics? It was Gloria herself who had brought the text-book to me in order to point out the author's error in that he had written 'I have done it' instead of the correct 'I done it'. Furthermore, Gloria insisted that the negative should be 'I ain't done it'—a phrase with which she was singularly familiar, and its close relation, 'I ain't done nothing' in the context of misdemeanours.

Sometimes Gloria was late for my class because she had popped into the toilet for a cigarette. She invariably apologized, assuring me that English was her favourite subject, presumably on the principle of the loving mother who murders her baby.

"Have you got a pen, sir?"

"Yes thank you, Gloria. I have a typewriter too."

"I mean can I lend it, sir?"

"My typewriter?"

"Oh, sir, I mean can I borry your pen! I'll give you a sweet if you do."

"Do what, Gloria?"

Gloria laughed delightedly at our little repartee, bending

over my desk so that her left breast accidentally filled my right eye socket. I said nothing, always being grateful for large mercies, but Gloria's bust created quite a hazard in the classroom, similar to an accident black spot on a busy road. For example, when she brought me a pile of books I had to be careful to take only the books from her, and when she was reading *Jane Eyre* she appeared to use her bust to keep the pages down, like paperweights. On one occasion when there had been a congestion in the corridor and I was pushing one class back to permit another class to exit I discovered too late that I was shunting Gloria back on the train-buffer principle.

In appearance Gloria had reached the peak of female perfection, in that not only was she beautiful all the way up but she was ideally proportioned. So perfect, in fact, that one sensed it could not last long, just as a rose must fade. Our girls reached their peak at varying ages; I recall Gwen Smith entering the classroom for the first time like a cover girl—long shiny hair, dimples, jewellery, nail varnish, slender legs in tights and stiletto heels which gave her a hippy wiggle—claiming to be twelve years old. Seating her among the little boys working on *The Selfish Giant,* I ran down to the office to check if this tall miss with the handbag had been directed to me in error, only to learn that today was actually her twelfth birthday.

Gloria attended school equipped with the affluence of the Welfare State, except for a pen. Her handbag contained a transistor radio, twenty No. 6 cigarettes; a packet of sweets and a comprehensive make-up repair yard from eye-wideners to barrier cream and deodorant. Her hair, which she brushed in class once per lesson, hung down her back like a silken veil, and her lemon dress was shorter than those worn for tennis. The ensemble was perched on high platform slingbacks she managed to walk on at £8.95. How extraordinary, I mused, that they actually pay me to teach these gorgeous dolls.

"How old are you, Gloria?" I inquired. Modern fashion

blurred her age to anything from fourteen to twenty-five.

"I'm sixteen, sir—today. Dad's going to take me to St Tropez in the holidays as a birthday present."

Crowhurst was on it in a flash. "You'll have to give her a kiss for her birthday, sir," he challenged me.

The class stared expectantly to see if I would rise to the occasion or bait, so, cunningly, I raised her hand to my lips, but before I could complete the operation Gloria put her arms round my neck and kissed me. I now appreciated why Gloria had been placed in my class because she could not get on with women teachers. Furthermore, upon taking her hand I had found myself staring at an engagement ring given her by Able Seaman Titmouse, now serving his country on board HMS *Everready*—one of those unsinkable men-o-war lying at anchor in the heart of the Welsh mountains.

On her wrist was the odd legend, 'I love Mike', just below an inked declaration that 'I love Manchester United'. On the other wrist we learned that 'I love Toenail Pie—True', an esoteric reference to a pop group rather than school dinners.

Long acquaintance with Gloria convinced me she loved everything even vaguely masculine, showing an unnatural zest in History for the great courtesans of the past, and describing minute life forms in Biology as Micro-Orgasms. The careers master told me confidentially that when the time came for Gloria to fill in her Youth Employment form he anticipated she would enter under Choice of job the words: 'Shop Assistant or Usherette, selling oranges at Drury Lane Playhouse. Or Au Pair girl at the court of Louis XIV'.

I was concerned with the effects of English Literature on Gloria, and had done my best to screen her from *The Song of Soloman* and *Rape of the Fair Country,* both of which were on our syllabus. The reason was that in her essays she was often employed by people like Lord Byron and Samuel Pepys, with the result that page two revealed her big with child or in an interesting condition, leading to page three where she entered suckling a man-child at her breast, or supporting her first-born while the Archbishop of Canterbury placed the crown of England on its wobbly head.

Moeover, I was not too happy about her favourite line of dialogue being read by the CSE Examination Board: 'My son is a little bastard but I love him dearly, even if he ain't King, and what I done I done and wants to do again soon, though it starts a bloody war between our Nights and them Wog Nights under the mighty Salad Tin'.

Crowhurst's buck teeth were sparkling with glee. "Naughty sir kissed Gloria!" he cried triumphantly, waving a card under my nose.

"Just for the record, Crowhurst, Gloria kissed me."

"No sir, you kissed Gloria. I can prove it—look ! "

Unbelievingly I stared at the photograph of Gloria and me in close embrace against the background of my blackboard, with Gloria on tiptoe so that she appeared to be all legs.

"It's his Polaroid camera, sir," Philip Webb explained, who always treated me as though I was feeble-minded and incapable of grasping modern technology.

"What a lovely clear picture!" I said feebly, trying to treat it like Salisbury Cathedral from Old Sarum.

"I shall enter it for the school camera club competition, sir. What a change from The Gym at Sunset. Must take first prize."

As my mind grappled with this horrific threat I was interrupted by one of the normal incidents of school life. Philip Webb approached me with his hand up. "Please sir, I laughed so much when you saw the photo that I swallowed me dinner token."

Philip's monotonous tone of voice indicated that his problem was not swallowing the little plastic coin so many of the pupils kept in their mouths like Polo Mints but disqualification from the dinner queue.

"Go to the office immediately, Philip," I commanded. This

department handled both first-aid and the issue of dinner tokens, so I was covered legally.

"Please sir, Linda's collapsed!" Debra informed me.

"Is it a fit?"

"No sir. She's a diabetic and ain't eaten her biscuits."

Now I remembered that if Linda didn't have her biscuits on the hour she was liable to drop dead at your feet—yet despite this she often forgot to take them. Gathering Linda's body in my arms I rushed her to the office, where Philip was already being treated for dinner tokens, almost colliding with a boy being carried out on a stretcher with a broken arm.

"Dance Drama, sir," Philip explained mysteriously, but I was in no mood to learn how one broke limbs in Dance Drama, especially as only girls took that subject. If the stretcher had been unoccupied I might have lain on it myself. Only last year one of our boys had fractured his leg during Religious Knowledge, so I was not flabbergasted at the news. Experience had taught me that children who were dying or had been seriously wounded in action on Mondays were usually as fit as sin on Tuesdays.

Returning to the classroom to start a belated lesson—and to relieve Crowhurst of the blackmail photograph by force if necessary—I ordered the class to produce their homework essay on the Novel. Gloria's essay favoured the Stuart period, which had gripped her imagination since she read *Strumpet Voluntary,* and she saw herself as top mistress of the year to Charles the Second. Once again I asked myself what the examiners would think when they checked her course work folder and read her opening sentence: 'My son is a little bastard but I love him dearly. . . .'

"Please sir, I'm writing my own novel," Crowhurst announced smugly. "I worked so long on it Sunday that I fell asleep mowing the lawn."

"Oh, good." This was my standard non-committal reply to Crowhurst, registering neither approval nor disapproval nor even interest.

"It's entitled Go Jump, sir."

"Oh, good."

"I expect you're wondering how I found such an unusual title, sir."

"No I'm not.

"Well, sir just as *Nunc Dimittis* is the title of the canticle in Luke ii because they are the first two words, so *Go Jump* are the first two words of what you often say to me, sir—'Go jump in the lake, Crowhurst'."

"Oh, good."

"I've used the same idea for chapter headings, sir. *'Get Lost', 'Drop Dead', "Button Up', 'Disappear Fishface',* and lots more. I'm always telling my dad about you, sir, and he reads all your books from the dockyard library. My mum says you're the funniest writer since Marie Stopes."

"Marie Stopes! She dealt with birth control."

"My mum says it's through you she's in the club again."

"What club?"

"The pudding club, sir. She was reading your book in bed, *Pook's Tale of Woo,* and it put her in such a good mood that she let dad woo her, sir. Pollination, sir."

It was noticeable how all the children tried to shield me from the facts of life. They would never let me see any nude pictures they found in *Art Through The Centuries* in the school library, they blocked my ears if they uttered a naughty word, and did their best to screen my eyes from risque passages in the set novels. What, I often wondered, would their reaction have been to see me formerly working as a part-time barman in a Shanghai bordello in order to pay the rent on my girl's flat? Or hiding from the German paratroops in a Crete brothel under the protection of seventeen young ladies of the town?

"Dad says your books ought to be on the National Health, sir."

"Oh, good."

"He reckons they have cured his constipation, sir."

This worried me because, although I sometimes received letters from readers that the books had cheered them up or postponed suicide, a lady had written only last week to say how, when all medical science had failed, I had ended her chronic insomnia. 'For years I suffered sleepless nights, but ever since a fellow victim recommended your books to me I have been unable to keep awake. Now, thanks to you, I enjoy deep refreshing slumber, even by day. In fact, this friend and I have a little joke about it by saying to each other "How did you Pook last night?" Then we reply, "I Pooked all night till the alarm went off".'

"My dad says you ought to be able to write well enough by now to do a proper novel, sir, just like real authors can. You know, with a plot and lots of four-letter words and everybody at it all the time with nothing on. Sex, sir."

"Oh, good."

"My novel is all about sex in schools, sir—that's why I wanted that picture of you and Gloria."

"Ye gods!"

"You see, sir, the girls don't seem to go for me."

"If it's any consolation, Crowhurst, it's not just the girls."

"Even Gloria don't like me, sir; she says I'm poofy and creepy."

"So she's not just a pretty face."

"In fact, sir, you're the best friend I've got in the school."

"I wouldn't put a lot of money on that, Crowhurst—you wouldn't bet on a racehorse that's in foal."

Crowhurst bared the teeth that propped up his thick lips, so I knew he was smiling archly. "So I'm writing a book about a school where you can do what comes naturally, even the teachers."

"Oh, a murder story?"

"No, sir—pollination."

"Tell me, Crowhurst, surely when the time comes you won't take your bride to the church and ask the vicar to pollinate you at a fertilization ceremony? You're not a blessed bee."

"There won't be time for marriage, sir, being an author. So far I've only done forty-seven pages."

"Why, have you been poorly?"

"I've put Gloria in the story, sir. I fancies her in that split skirt."

Gloria was trendy but she did not seem to believe in the mystery of womanhood. Fashion decreed a split skirt, on the assumption that one wore a skirt to split. Somehow Gloria had managed to introduce a split into her token skirt, revealing a tantalizing glimpse of hockey bruise, and when she bent over she revealed a tantalizing panorama of her bottom. I pretended not to notice a heart sewn on this region which bore the legend: 'Pants Down for Bunny Brown'—obviously the slogan of her current pop idol.

Mr Figgin, the metalwork master, entered the room unexpectedly. "Ah, Pook, the caretaker tells me you have an obsolete radiator here," he chuckled.

"Yes, over there between the windows."

A steel rule appeared like an extension to Mr Figgin's arm. "Just the right size too," he mused, measuring height and length with one hand. An adjustable spanner materialized from his apron, there was a metallic clink from two pipes, then the old radiator slid from the wall and Mr Figgin carried it bodily from the room. It struck me how, even as he freed the radiator, Mr Figgin did not look at his work. Instead, his eyes swept the walls and ceiling for signs of metal.

"What are you going to do with it, Mr Figgin?" I queried.

"Keep Britain tidy, Peter. Ah, what's that retractable bracket doing on your ceiling?"

"I think it once supported a globe of the world when this was the Geography room," I replied, noting how Mr Figgin spoke to you without looking at you because you weren't metal.

Suddenly Mr Figgin was standing on a desk, ratchet-screwdriver in one hand and my bracket in the other, like a conjuring trick.

"Thanks, Peter, just what I needed for the mainmast," he said, still not looking at me, but this time with his head in my stock-cupboard. "Ah, I don't suppose you ever use that old filing-cabinet."

Instinctively I stood between the cabinet and Mr Figgin, arms outspread to protect my own. "I do, I do—all the time."

"Pity. Beautiful roller-bearings under the drawers in that model. Well, I'll be off."

I opened the door for Mr Figgin rather than let him handle the brass knob, and bade him good-bye. Mr Franklin once told me that when Dr Collins had finally decided to trade his magnificent 1948 Rover Twelve, with walnut door tops and leather upholstery, Mr Figgin was observed by Mr Franklin from the staff room window to strip off the caravan tow-unit. But this was merely the butcher whetting his knife preparatory to the main cut. Both Mr Figgin and Mr Tadd were under the car, so Mr Franklin knew there was a bigger job on, like an engine or a chassis.

Mr Franklin declared that when the Headmaster eventually drove off with the car salesman for the deal, he witnessed an extraordinary sight. The Rover left behind on the school car park the built-in jacking system for all four wheels.

Even today the notice board bears a faded appeal, signed by Dr Collins, asking if any member of staff had borrowed or knew the whereabouts of the school gates. These double gates at the entrance were never swung to or used in any way, with the result that they were not missed until the Headmaster happened to notice one day that the lugs on the twin brick pillars were supporting nothing. By consulting an old photograph of the opening ceremony being performed by the Mayor of Cudford,

Dr Collins was able to check the design of the gates, but in doing so he discovered that originally the brick pillars had been surmounted by the twin torches of Learning and Enterprise, both of which had apparently burnt themselves out and disappeared.

Since then Dr Collins had been perusing old photographs in an attempt to find out just how much of the school had vanished, like geographers study Britain's west coast for erosion by the sea. Moreover he had taken the precaution to have the school premises photographed, including the roofs. This followed his announcement at Assembly that the timber Rural Studies building was to be demolished during half-term and replaced by a brick structure. When the contractors arrived to demolish it they were surprised to find it had gone. In fact, they could only locate the site by the footings and some broken glass. This unsolved mystery coincided with the laying down of the keel for the ketch *Lucky Break,* and the introduction of Mr Tadd's new course for ROSLA pupils who now had to stay at school for the extra year called 'Try Your Hand'. As a direct result of 'Try Your Hand' Dr Collins' study was losing some of its light and all its view as a wooden boathouse gradually arose outside his window.

Under pressure of the ROSLA emergency he had sanctioned a shed for storing our canoes on racks, but the shed never seemed to stop growing as forty boys were instructed in the art of building a shed capable of accommodating *Lucky Break* and the new motor sloop *Rosla the First,* side by side.

Soon Dr Collins was further reminded about the raising of the school leaving age to sixteen, for he sat in his study listening to the day-long hammering and sawing as Mr Figgin and Mr Tadd directed their new labour force in boatbuilding as though Dr Collins was running a Clydeside shipyard instead of a school. In fact, there was a strong feeling in the staff room that Messrs Tadd and Figgin were actually selling boats on the open market—a feeling which increased when Dr Collins was watching television one night and saw *Rosla the First* on display at the Earls Court Boat Show.

Outside in the car park six members of staff had cars there with boats secured behind on trailers, giving the place the air of a yacht marina, but what really made Dr Collins sit in his study and mop his brow was our training ship, *Spirit of Adventure.* Puzzled why she had not yet been employed in the ROSLA scheme, Dr Collins went down to the river on a tour of inspection. He boarded her by the starboard gangplank, only to discover his way barred by a rope and an explanatory sign which read: 'Danger. No decks'. The Headmaster stared in disbelief straight down to the keelson. Then his eyes swept across the beam of the vessel to the port side—but there was no port side. Only the timber ribs framing a panoramic view of the river and a distant prospect of Liddale Farm.

"My oath, only half a ship left!" Dr Collins cried. "Less than half! I demand to know where it has gone to. Mr Tadd, how do you account for this . . . this skeleton of my ship?"

"Here is your answer, sir," Mr Tadd replied, placing in the Headmaster's hand a one-ounce tobacco tin containing wood dust and a dried-up beetle. That's the little fellow to blame."

Dr Collins put on his reading glasses, the better to examine the tiny corpse which had eaten his ship down to the keelson.

"Anobium punctatum, sir, assisted by his cousin Xestobium rufovillosum—the same couple who did the *Victory* at Portsmouth," Mr Tadd added, as if referring to a firm of Italian shipbreakers.

"Don't show me bugs, man—I want to know where half my training ship has disappeared to! The *Victory* didn't vanish when the Captain of the Dockyard went to lunch."

"This should put your mind at rest, sir," Mr Figgin said, handing Dr Collins a small glass slide with nothing on it. "Look closely and you will observe in the centre a spore of merulius lachrymans, that deadly fungus known as dry-rot—the sailor's nightmare. It has been our painful duty to shack out the infected timbers in order to save the ship, sir."

"Save what ship? There's no ship to save, man! For weeks I was under the impression I saw her lying down by the river, but now I realize it was merely a façade, only the starboard side."

"Well, sir, now you have seen the condition she's in you will appreciate why the starboard side will have to be shacked out," Mr Figgin observed calmly. "Highly dangerous to life and limb, sir—just watch this."

Mr Figgin picked up the baulk of timber which was always placed behind Dr Collins during his inspections, hit it with a four-pound hammer, then watched Dr Collins disappear in a cloud of wood powder, as though he had walked into a fog bank. Because the Head was a martyr to hay fever he was obliged to retreat from *The Spirit of Adventure* at the double, his mind preoccupied with thoughts far from academic.

TEN

"Don't read my poem out to the class, will you, sir," Gloria begged, handing me her poetry folder on which she had inscribed the title POTERY. The folder contained nearly a hundred poems Gloria had composed in her own time, painstakingly indexed under the heading of POEMTRY, ninety-six of which revealed the intimate details of her love life, plus one devoted to her first-born man-child.

It was difficult to know whether Gloria's request meant me to read her poem aloud or not, but experience had taught me that if I obeyed her plea and respected her privacy she tended to sulk. Gloria's method of handing me her folder represented the extreme in teacher-pupil rapport. She invariably walked out to the front of the class with the folder in one hand, then slid her free arm round my waist and suddenly collapsed on my chest, so that I found myself with an unsuspected amount of coeducation in my arms. While leaning her head on my breast she had an unhygienic habit of dribbling down my tie, simultaneously expressing a morbid fancy that "I wish you was my dad, sir."

Today I had a strong premonition that I heard the click of a concealed Polaroid camera just as the tiny plastic flower atop Gloria's hair-band went up my nostril.

"Gosh, I'm hot, sir," Gloria said without moving.

"You never ought to be, dear. . . ." I stopped short rather than risk misunderstanding by adding that anyone with as little on as she should be shivering, because Gloria's mode of dress gave people the impression that she came to school wearing only a smock and platform shoes. Once in fun I had warned her that if she chatted the boys up in class I would make her stand on the chair. She immediately did this, and the resultant whistles from the boys at so much leg made me pull her down in panic.

"This time I've written a pome all about love, sir," Gloria informed me, as though normally she wrote about fire-engines.

"It's called 'When Will It Happen To Me?'" Rather than answer this obvious question I asked Gloria to put me down so I could read the poem to the class. She retired delighted to her desk and tried to look shy.

> I always love the boys, even when they make a noise.
> I'll love Mike until I die, even though he makes me cry.
> Once when he gave me flowers tears ran down my
>   cheeks in showers,
> As I wept for hours and hours.
> But I shall love him till I die, and the Angles take us to
>   the sky,
> Because I have given him my heart, and told him we must
>   never part.

My rendering of the poem was greeted by the class with a tumultuous silence, as if they were stunned by grief for Mike, though to be fair to Gloria this was standard reception for all poetry, whether by Crowhurst or William Blake.

"That was very nice and extremely nauseating, Gloria," I said, exploiting vocabulary to give her praise, yet vindicating my conscience by using an adjective she would not understand. I was not too happy about her space-probe Angles, though doubtless they were Right Angles, but remembering Gloria's spelling of Volcadbury, in which she insisted that her mum scalded her for washing the telly with a boy to whom she had been interjuiced by a maiden Ant whose christian name was Sonyer, when that lady took her to see the Loins of Longleat, I said nothing.

"I can do better than that, sir," Jim Maynard advised the class. "I done one called 'Ode to a Gas-meter'. See, sir, take the money out of a gas-meter—'Owed to a Gas-meter'."

"Why don't you draw me a picture too, Jim?" I retorted, piqued by this general impression that I was a qualified idiot.

"And turn round, Crowhurst—it frightens the others."

Some of the girls could write remarkably vivid and sensitive poetry, but I had to be wary of Jim Maynard ever since he wrote 'Leopard, Leopard Burning Bright'. My suspicions were aroused immediately I spotted words like Halcyon Days or Multitudinous Seas Incamadine. Surely now I was not going to get Shelley's 'Ode to a Gas-meter'?—commencing 'Hail to thee, blithe money burner, how I longs to force you open'.

The class listened apathetically to the familiar tale of Maynard doing a gas-meter in rhyme while his unsuspecting dad lay drunk on the kitchen floor. At its conclusion I commented that his work was efficient and extremely pernicious, which he assumed was high praise.

Gloria put her hand up to ask a question, looking at me archly from the tops of her eyes. "Please sir, I'm sixteen today. Do you know what that means?"

"You are no longer fifteen?"

"No, sir, there's something special about a girl reaching sixteen."

"You mean in the eyes of the law?"

"Oh, sir, you are naughty! I mean me and Mike can get married."

"How exciting." Surprising how quickly the class tired of poetry, I reflected.

"Although I got engaged when I was fourteen, Mum wouldn't let me have the party till now."

"Listen to her and you'll end up an embittered old maid."

"So will you come, sir? Here's an official invitation card, RSVP, then I'll send you an invitation to the wedding."

"Is that on the same day or are you going to have a long engagement till the following Saturday?"

My heart sank to think I must attend another such function, where everybody sat on the floor throughout the house, deafened by pop music, drink in one hand, cigarette in the other, staring into space. The lucky ones were jammed in the living-room where they could watch television, though not hear it. At the last engagement party I attended I sat on the stairs watching the clock.

"Yes, I'd love to come, Gloria."   A teacher has to be dedicated.

"Oh fab, sir. I hope you can stay all night."

This was unlikely, for I had developed a technique where I delivered the present, met the parents, kissed the bride-to-be, took a drink, then visited the toilet and disappeared into the silence of the night via the garden wall.

"Another thing about a girl's sixteenth birthday, sir, is that she's allowed to do anything she likes."

"She likes you, sir," Crowhurst sniggered.

"There are limits to birthday privilege, Gloria."

"Let's give her the bumps."

"She's already got 'em."

"Then why don't she strip off?"

Once again I was struggling to get the class, if not back to poetry, at least off their favourite topic.   The other girls, immaculate with their bright dresses and long sleek tresses, looked on smilingly but detached, like mothers watching other people's children at play.

"What I really mean, sir, is that I don't have to do no work on my birthday, see?"

"But then your birthday would be like any other day in the year, Gloria."

"Oh, sir, you are dinnie!" she giggled. I used to think dinnie was a corruption of the Scottish dinnle, which means thrilling, but I had since learnt it was a school word for the mentally retarded. The children did not often call me dinnie, preferring another word with a subtle shade of meaning—nutty.

During break I employed my own teaching method of picking a rose from outside the staff room window and presenting it to Gloria. "To beauty the rose, dear," I explained hastily, seeing from her expression that she thought the class had to compose a poem about roses.

"Oh sir, I wish you was my dad," she sighed, collapsing on my chest for a quick dribble, while I wondered how her dad got on for ties. "Have a sweet for being such a nice teacher."

"Late detention, sir!" the class cried triumphantly. "Mustn't eat in class, sir!"

"Why should I be the only one not eating then?"

"I'm not eating in class, sir," Crowhurst informed me smugly.

"Creep!" I discovered too late that I myself had called him this name. "Now, class, back to poetry, please."

Crowhurst stood up. "Please sir, I've done an epic."

"Was a poem too difficult for you?"

"An epic is better than a poem, sir—it's heroic."

"Big-'ead!" Once more I felt ashamed to find it was I who had made the remark to Crowhurst.

"What's more, it don't rhyme, sir—like real poetry. All about a stallion named Rebel. Can I read it to the class, sir?"

"Only you know if you can; I merely say that you may."

Crowhurst grinned at having ousted Gloria from the limelight and brushed his black fringe clear of his spectacles. "'Rebel', by yours truly me—ha, ha!; Poet Laureate. . . ."

"Get on with it, Fish-head."

"'Framed by lightning,
Lit by flashes against the storm-torn sky,
Rebel doubled the thunder rumble with hooves that drummed
The ground, drummed the ground, drummed the pounded ground.
A black blur of power streaking across the moorland,
Rain-shone flanks pulsating under the rhythm of his legs,

Like the Devil's stallion fire-spewed from Hell
To bestride the heavens via the land of hiding men.
Against the exploding sky I saw Rebel's mane fly back
Flag-stiff from his noble head—
That proud head punctured by the wide white wild eye
Which blinked not in its course across the moor,
Nor heeded me the least—yet I could not stare it out.
That wide white wild eye so fiery I must tremble to
   behold
This Devil's Derby racing from the starting-gate of
   Hell
To the end of the world at Judgement Day.
Methinks it haunts me to the grave, that wide white
   wild eye
Of Rebel blazing like a meteor across the track of time
   and space,
And I a poor spectator of the cosmic race."

Crowhurst's oration was greeted with an outburst of
spontaneous indifference by the class, so I said, "Remembering
our work on Poetry Appreciation, may we have comments,
please?"

"It's all right," Gloria observed.

"Orright," Maynard agreed.

"Same as him," Margaret added.

"Orright. Bit long though," Linda decided.

Next to Religious Knowledge, Poetry was certainly the dead
horse of this school, I reflected, at the same time racking my
memory to trace where Crowhurst had plagiarized 'Rebel'. The
lines were vaguely familiar, yet I could not place them nor the
style.

"That's a cert for the school magazine, sir," Crowhurst
remarked, buck teeth at the grin. He had noticed the impact of
the poem on me, so was prepared to make hay while the sun

shone, employing a combine harvester. "None of your June-Moon-Soon rubbish there, sir, but figures of speech, vivid use of vocab, alliteration, metaphors, similes, onomatopoeia, verbal repetition, personification, final rhyming couplet, Shakespeare's sensual W, effective word-combinations—the lot. Just like you gave us in our poetry notes, sir. CSE Grade One coming up, sir!"

"Are you positive you wrote it yourself, Crowhurst?"

"You have my word as Poet Laureate, sir. Goes to show what a hot teacher you are, sir."

"Can you explain your use of the word Cosmic in the last line?"

"Not offhand, sir. It's all in my notes though."

"May I see your notes, please?"

"Ah, they're at home, sir. My dad's doing your Poetry course too."

"Did he help you with the poem?"

"Dad! He couldn't rhyme Above with Love, sir. Ha, ha!"

"So this is your own unaided work?"

"Of course, sir. You told us how much tripe was spouted about the genius of poetry—inspiration and visions and spiritual communion with Nature and all that. You said composing poetry was just another mechanical process like any other creative work, sir. Hard graft and persistence did it, sir, not the inner soul and emotional revelations and all that, you said. You said Shakespeare didn't search his subconscious for the plays and sonnets, sir—he sat in a London workshop and slogged at the business of earning a living as a playwright. You said all that bunk about pouring out his libido under some sort of divine inspiration was invented later by blokes who wouldn't admit that a commoner done it all by hard work and natural talent."

"You said Shakespeare put Anne Hathaway in the club, sir," Gloria added. "Will you really come to my wedding, sir?"

"Gloria, I will indeed. Now please try to concentrate on the lesson, but if you want my personal opinion you are too young for marriage—you don't give yourself a chance to see life before you settle down. By the time you've got two youngsters your husband will realize it as well, then he'll be off to pastures new. That's why I'm second dad to half the kids here."

Gloria looked indignant. "But, sir, you said that when Mohammed married his favourite wife Ayesha she was only nine."

"So now I suppose you're grumbling at missing the best seven years of your married life? Anyway, that was back in the seventh century."

"You said Charles the Second had so many mistresses that they had to be numbered like footballers, sir. You said King Solomon had 360 wives, sir. I like History because I could have been Alexander the Great's concubine, sir."

I had long discovered the futility of appealing to history for moral example, where every period we covered made today's permissive society sound like an Olde Tyme Dancing class. Nor had I recovered from Gloria's reaction when I was explaining to the class how, in certain confined regions with a limited food area—such as in mountainous settlements and island communities—it was economically essential to practise polyandry. When Gloria heard that polyandry involved one woman taking several husbands it seemed she had discovered her life's work, and she asked me if one could visit such places on a Poly Tour package holiday.

"If I lived in Georgia, sir, I could have married Mike when I was fourteen," Gloria persisted.

"Poetry, dear—remember? Consult your notes."

"De Quincey, Byron, Swinburne, Wilde—who's this bloke, sir?—Saucer . . . Chaucer."

"No, I don't think we'll tackle any of those today, class," I chuckled, searching my mind for any poet without the sort of erotic background that knocks a teacher off his feet. "Let us turn to page 315, good old safe Wordsworth and his 'Daffodils'."

If you weren't safe with 'The Daffodils' and 'Yarrow Revisited' you might as well pack up. Samuel Butler had said of a certain puritanical writer that 'He was capable of bringing out an expurgated edition of Wordsworth', and Joseph Short-house once remarked of the poems that 'Wordsworth's standard of intoxication was miserably low', so I was on firm ground at last.

Gloria read her green fingernails to attract my attention. "Please sir, is this the same bloke what you said put Marie-Anne Vallon in the club when he went to France in 1791?"

"For G——... ah, there goes the dinner bell, class. Books away till tomorrow, when we shall be looking at a poet you've never heard of before—I hope—Hesiod, 800 B.C., who wrote about farming in Greece."

Determined to find its source I hawked the poem 'Rebel' round the staff room, with little success. This was unusual because most problems could be solved by someone on our staff of sixty teachers, from mathematics to income tax, and from archaeology to air-brakes. Only Mr Whittle thought he recognized it as the early work of the modern Russian poet Vladimir Kussevitzky, circa 1934, during his black period, when, under the influence of the Ural Poets led by Sergeyevich Kramatorsky, he experimented in expressing the spirit of the revolution through the metamorphosis of animals in conflict with the elements, such as a stallion combating the storm in the poem under review.

What made Whittle doubly certain was the presence of Kussevitzky's characteristic *raison d'être,* the overthrow of evil by man through the cathartic intervention of natural forces sublimated to the will of the people, despite man's timidity to exploit them to the full because of social and economic controls inhibiting his obvious environmental advantages.

One thing was certain, Kussevitzky or not, Crowhurst had not written it.

Whittle returned from our library with *Modern Soviet Poets and Kramatorsky's Riddle,* while Dr Collins himself produced from his study the definitive work on Kussevitzky, *What Did He Mean?* But none of them referred to 'Rebel'. The mystery so obsessed Whittle that he worked right through Russian literature until he got back in time to 1760, now positive that the poem had come from the pen of Mikhail Lomonosov during his struggle to establish an effective Russian language freed from the bonds of formal Slavonic.

Unfortunately, Mr Dorsett of our English Department declared that the poem was about as Russian as a frankfurter sausage, and that anybody other than a highly-trained idiot could tell that it was the work of the German Expressionism school in the shape of Georg Trakl. To prove his point Mr Dorsett opened the definitive volume *What, Why—and If,* and after a day's search he was able to confirm what we had all suspected, that the poem 'Rebel' was not mentioned anywhere.

Mr Figgin stated that because the poem was not connected with the sea he did not recognize it, but Miss Shampoo declared it not to be a poem at all because poetry was an abstract conception, a delusion of the mind, therefore, like love, did not exist in factual terms. Dr Collins held confidently that the poem was the work of his late friend Professor Cable, of Cudford University, who, at the advanced age of ninety-six, had been certified to be of unsound mind until further examination led to the diagnosis that he was probably dead.

I remember attending Professor Cable's lectures at the College of Education, where I first heard his celebrated precept, 'In order to teach, one must teach', and his famous Induction Speech: "I can't tell you how to teach; nobody here can tell you how to teach. I can't tell you what to teach; nobody here can tell you what to teach. I can't tell you what teaching is; nobody here can tell you what teaching is. I can't tell you whom to teach; nobody here can tell you whom to teach. And this is the torch we pass on to you, this glorious tradition of not knowing why we teach, nor what it is, nor how to do it, certain in the knowledge that our trust in you is not misplaced, and that as educational theories are constantly changed you will stand steadfast as a rock in a sea of uncertainty by not knowing if they are good or bad."

Realizing by now that the solution would have to come from Crowhurst, I interviewed him in my classroom alone and I employed modern educational technique. Because today there is no effective punishment for doing what was once thought wrong, except by diminution of reward, I held the reward behind my back in the form of a half-pound block of Galaxy chocolate. I showed it casually to Crowhurst as I spoke kindly to him.

"There's an argument going on in the staff room, Crowhurst, about who really wrote that poem 'Rebel'."

"I done it, sir," he replied apprehensively.

"We know you did, lad, but forget that. This has nothing to do with lessons; just an answer to settle a kind of quiz, you might say. Give me the answer and here's a nice big bar of chocolate for telling the truth."

"Suppose I don't, sir?"

"So you don't, that's all. Of course, you won't get the full bar of chocolate. As a sort of punishment you'll only get half, or even less."

"Will you be mad, sir?"

"Me? Heavens no, Crowhurst, why should I be mad? I shall understand. Everybody is entitled to plead the Fifth Amendment. Who cares about a silly old poem anyway? If I appear to take you in the stock-cupboard when there are no witnesses about and knock your teeth out and say you fell off the ladder onto your face, that will be sheer coincidence. Strike lucky with a magistrate and he might accept my word against yours."

Crowhurst's guilty look made me feel ashamed of my conduct and extremely glad. "I honestly don't know who writ it, sir," he confessed. "That's the truth, so can I have the bar of chocolate?"

As a punishent I gave him only half the bar for not telling the whole truth. I appreciated this was wrong of me under the circumstances, but sometimes one has to be cruel to be kind. To be on the safe side, Crowhurst began to eat his punishment in case I changed my mind.

"Let's have it, lad," I coaxed, astonished at the rapid disposal of chocolate through his thick lips which a plumber might use to unblock a sink.

"I don't know, honest, sir. Remember how I wanted a ring folder for my project and you gave me an old one from your cupboard? You said throw the papers away, sir, but instead of that I kept them and read 'em. One was all about a unicorn called Noble belting across the world, so I just changed the unicorn to a horse and called him Rebel. That's the truth, sir, so can I have the other half of my punishment now, please?"

I handed Crowhurst the half-bar of Galaxy without speaking, for I was far away back at College, handing my poem 'Noble' to old Professor Cable. He gradually took it from me, then slowly clipped on the bifocals to peruse the title when he had found the range down by his knees, and I had placed a finger by the N in order to give him a sighting mark.

"That is my assignment poem 'Noble', sir," I shouted into his left ear, in case he thought it was the evening paper.

"Ho ho, young man, then let us hope it is a noble poem, eh? A noble poem, ha, ha, ha, ha, ha! I must remember to tell Dame May Boyle that one—a noble poem, what!"

"I expect there's a pun there somewhere, sir. The poem is about a unicorn."

"A uniform, young man? A naval uniform or an army uniform?"

"About a naval unicorn called Buttons, sir. It gallops around till it finds an officer to jump on."

"About a naval uniform, young man? Dame May Boyle will be extremely interested to learn how you fitted a naval uniform into our theme of mythological animals."

"It wasn't easy, sir; I had to cut the sleeves off."

This was standard dialogue with Professor Cable, which saved time and energy, and my being sent out to purchase a new battery for his hearing-aid. I worked it on the principle of two parties to a phone conversation, neither of whom realizes he has been cut off.

"Tell me, young man, before you go, have you read my book, *What is Poetry?*"

"No, sir, but I saw the film."

"Neither do I, young man. I have yet to meet anybody who can tell me what poetry really is. Here am I, an emeritus Professor of Poetry, yet all my life I have been asking what it is. I don't know what it is, Pook; no one here can tell you what it is. Frankly, it has been one of the many mysteries of this world I have failed to solve. All I ask of you is that you will never pin me down by saying, 'Professor Cable, what is poetry?'"

"Life is too short, sir. Teach it!" I bellowed the last two words into the Professor's left ear as a verbal cue-card to remind him that he was required to show me how to teach poetry to children.

"Or you may be tempted to inquire of me how one teaches the subject. My reply would be quite frank; I don't know. As I mentioned to Dame May Boyle, how can one teach something when one does not know what it is? I myself have tried to do so and failed lamentably, because poetry can only be experienced, not taught. It cannot be analysed, dissected, examined nor comprehended, young man. One may as well be asked to teach the Mona Lisa or a summer rose or the tang of the ocean."

Professor Cable always made me feel that my new career was impossible, but at least it seemed that my own poem was secure from any form of censure, like modern art. Yet I missed the ancient scholar when people started to talk amongst themselves that he had deceitfully passed away behind their backs without notifying the class. He had been discovered in close perusal of his notes on his study desk, buried in the manuscript of his contribution to the perennial Bacon-Marlowe controversy surrounding the authorship of Shakespeare's plays, entitled *Was the Bard Really Anne Hathaway?* This, of course, is the authoritative source of the celebrated literary cryptic: 'Was Hamlet a Danish Bacon'?

I gave Crowhurst the patriarchal smile based on Dr Collins' precept that one must seek out the good in every action, even if your throat has been slit. "Well done, Crowhurst, you have revived past memories for me by telling the truth."

"Can I have a merit mark for it, sir?"

"Certainly, lad—right between the eyes if you don't hand over those Polaroid snaps pronto."

"But they're mine, sir, for my project."

"I know, sonny, but as one blackmailer to another I'm sure you realize how some things are just not worth the price. Let's say I'm merely borrowing them to show my Nan, eh?"

"But Dr Collins wouldn't punish me, sir. He'd say my poem showed initiative in research and adaptation."

"Quite so, Crowhurst, but your dad might."

"My dad never punishes me, sir. He always takes my side."

"But he might if you had to show him your new camera and explain how a bus ran over it while you were photographing our lollipop lady outside the school gates."

"I take your point, sir."

As I pocketed the photographs Mr Mould looked in to invite me to form a two-man riot squad to quell a slight case of uproar in the History room and in the corridor adjoining it.

"It's the Fourth Years having a go with Lennie the Lion," Mr Mould explained as we hurried downstairs. Mr Leonard was our new Graduate History teacher straight from Cudford

University, whose nickname derived from his mane of hair and beard which left almost nothing visible below his glasses except a nose. He wore the trendy academic garb of sweater, jeans and a pair of abandoned plimsolls. The tightness of the jeans gave such a distended aspect to his rear that Mr Mould declared a desire to call the doctor to lance it.

Owing to disciplinary troubles Mr Leonard had adopted the unorthodox procedure of putting the boys outside in the corridor that he might better cope with the girls. Our school being what it was, twenty fifteen-year-olds unsupervised in a public place constituted a riotous assembly such as drove some women teachers to nervous breakdowns and some men teachers to quit the profession in favour of the tranquillity of the armed forces or industry.

"Lennie has been telling them they need no longer rebel against the oppression of Imperialist authority," Mr Mould continued en route, "because he is one of the people, and does not wish to exploit them as factory-fodder for Capitalist industry."

"Then why are they still rebelling, Mr Mould?"

"Because they won't give him a hearing. He's thrown the boys out so he can try to explain it to the girls. He kept them all in after school yesterday to tell them they were free now and could learn true History without fear of repression, but they started to wreck the classroom until he had to send for the Head."

Once Mr Mould and I had pulled Fred Rubble off Sandsod, the corridor riot subsided to near silence, broken only by the shouts of Mr Leonard within as he endeavoured to subdue the girls.

"Rubble, why were you hitting Sandsod?" Mr Mould demanded.

"Because he needled me, sir," Rubble growled. "Lennie said I was one of the workers now, so Sandsod shouted out that was impossible because I'm a skiving git like, didn't 'e."

"Listen, boys, another word out of anybody and wicked oppressive old Mouldy will bat you round the ear while Mr Pook kicks you up the corridor," Mr Mould warned severely. The boys giggled to hear their old warrior speak thus, but silence reigned. "You see, lads, it has been well said that violence begets violence; therefore when I witness Rubble doing over Sandsod, it is incumbent upon me to do over Rubble and Sandsod too. Rubble for fighting, Sandsod for losing.

"Me, sir!" Sandsod gasped.

"Yes, you, Sandsod. It takes two to start a bundle, but—far worse—you allowed yourself to get beaten up. No crime so abhorrent to me as defeat, boy. You deprived me of the pleasure of seeing Rubble busted and spread over—a delightful and picturesque colloquialism derived, I believe, from a dropped egg."

"Me, sir!" Rubble gasped. As always, the boys listened open-mouthed to Mr Mould's unorthodox rhetoric.

"Yes, you sir. You will appreciate my concern, Rubble, when I consider that only one year remains to me in which I may witness your being busted and spread over before your departure from the halls of learning to the arms of Social Security and Supplementary Benefits. The joy of your departure will provide scant recompense if you are permitted to leave us unspread and not done over. However, the moment you pass out of the gates next July you will no longer be a pupil in the eyes of the law—perhaps an opportune moment for an old man in the winter of life to gratify his last whim with the aid of a mask and a blackjack."

The boys listened spellbound to their old leader, convinced by his eloquence that he meant what he said, just as all pupils did. I recall the panic among the girls when the Senior Mistress addressed them about the state of their toilets—in which some of them defaced the walls, broke the mirrors and smoked the forbidden cigarette—and Mr Mould advised them that closed-circuit television was being installed to monitor their conduct therein. The effect of his announcement had such a deleterious influence on some of the guilty parties' waterworks—Gloria even attempted to use the boys' toilet in the lull during lesson time—that the Senior Mistress was obliged to issue a formal denial.

But Mr Mould's classic case occurred some years ago on April the First, when, discovering the switchboard deserted, he phoned every office and department the dread message that: 'Her Majesty's Inspectors of Schools have arrived on a surprise visit. They are presently touring the building, so you are requested not to leave your office or classroom until they enter to see you at work *in situ.*'

Whereupon a unique change fell upon the school. The teaching blocks became monastic in their silence, bee-like in their industry. The corridors were hushed and deserted, the toilet tanks flushed not, nor were heard the angry shouts of the staff like captains calling to captains across the smoke of an ancient battlefield. Even Dr Collins was trapped in his study, pen poised in toil, awaiting the fatal knock at his door, wondering where in the vast complex of buildings the enemy was located at any given moment.

Not until 12.15 did teachers begin to send out messengers to inquire if classes should be dismissed for lunch, even though the Inspectors had not yet got round to them. This was followed by a general search of the premises for the Inspectors by the staff, with a view to inviting them to the dining-hall for the midday meal. Of course, they were not found, and it took some time to question our staff of sixty for Dr Collins to discover that no one had seen them all morning, let alone been visited. Mr Mould judged from the mood of the staff that this was no time to shout 'April Fool!'—and prudently kept his secret for evermore.

"Why have you been playing up Mr Leonard, Sandsod?" Mr Mould demanded.

"'Cos the lessons is boring, sir."

"You mean he has run out of Tom-and-Jerry cartoons?"

"No sir; he keeps on about Russia saving us like they saved 'Ungry and Checkyslackyer."

"Oh indeed! Did Mr Leonard mention how the Red Army marched into Czechoslovakia in the nick of time to save the Czechs from conquering themselves?"

"I fink so, sir. There was so much racket I didn't hear much what he said."

"What else did he tell you?"

"He said we wasn't to call him Lennie the Lion, sir, but to use his own name of Brian."

"But according to the Fourth Year syllabus you are supposed to be learning local history—Cudford and its environs."

"We ain't done Cudford nor environs, sir. We ain't done nuffink really 'cept muck about. We 'ates him, sir."

Mr Mould turned to me. "Observe, Mr Pook, how children abhor the vacuum of so-called-freedom and despise attempts to abolish natural strata of age and ability. May the Lord in his wisdom preserve us and the children from what I choose to call the maritime convoy system, in which the speed of every ship is dictated by the speed of the slowest vessel. May the Lord in his wisdom preserve us from what I choose to call the flying circus pilots—those experts who soar high above the clouds in order to declare what we poor ants should do far below in the fields of education. Now let us override professional etiquette by going to our friend's assistance—not that it will have any lasting effect, because, *nota bene,* every teacher must stand on his own feet in the classroom."

"Shut up and sit down, the lot of you!" Mr Leonard was shrieking as we entered, but the girls ignored the command until they saw Mr Mould. Immediately, without further exhortation, they returned to their desks in silence.

Mr Mould smiled at them. "Good-morning, girls."

"Good-morning, sir."

"Excuse the intrusion, Mr Leonard, but I merely popped in to see if you would be so kind as to lend me a stick of chalk. Come in, lads—don't want you taking cold in a draughty corridor. That's good; sit there quietly with the girls. Forgive my mentioning this, Mr Leonard, but these are a difficult class sometimes—did I sense a slight unrest as I passed your door?"

Mr Leonard shook his mane ironically. "Hell's delight every time I take them. The little devils won't listen to me. All they want to do is muck about or fight."

"Well, it's boring, sir," Daphne Hyde interrupted unexpectedly. "He keeps on about what we don't know nothing about. Why do girls have to learn History, sir?"

"Why do girls have to learn Chemistry and Physics, sir?"

"My mum says school is a waste of time and I ought to be out earning some money."

"What good is Geography to me?—I got a job already."

"I'm getting married next year anyway."

"Margaret Brown's working down the market; that's why she don't never come to school."

"I got to stay on because I wants to be a nurse."

"My mum's going to get me a job in Cudford Box factory."

"Well, I likes school and I don't want to leave yet."

"My dad says if this is supposed to be a free country why can't we leave when we wants to?"

"I could be getting £20 a week now on a building site."

"I gets £2 just for Saturdays, down at General Butchers."

"I could leave this term if I was only one day older."

"My dad says we got to stay on because the Government don't want no more unemployed on the dole."

Mr Mould smiled at Mr Leonard. "Well, that's a fair cross-section of opinion, eh? Note how the job-money syndrome dominates their thinking rather than academic pursuit, similar to most adults. Allow me to answer them briefly, please."

Mr Leonard readily agreed, grateful for the respite and

surprised by the attentive atmosphere throughout the room. Mr Mould sat on Daphne Hyde's desk and patted her head affectionately.

"Are you eating in class, Daphne? '

"Yes, sir."

"Good. Remind me afterwards to keep you in—not for eating but for not giving me one."

Blushing, yet pleased by the attention, Daphne offered Mr Mould an old-fashioned humbug from a distinctly old-fashioned crumpled bag.

"Boys and girls, you have to stay at school until sixteen because the law says so—though personally I believe some would benefit by an earlier release; those of us who are so unsuited to the pursuit of learning that school is almost a form of unnecessary suffering. Why must girls learn this and that?— well, one can make a case for teaching them everything, or an equally good case for teaching them nothing. I suppose, like most things in life, we must compromise. However, I believe that Daphne here won't regret her education later on, because, besides her job, it should enable her to lead a happier, more interesting life, and should certainly help her give her own children a better start in life than perhaps she had herself."

Daphne—now imagining herself proud mother of six nodded vigorously, sure in the knowledge that whatever happened in the future her offspring could not possibly start worse off than she had to. I could sense how all the girls were making a mental note of this new aspect of education. They adored babies, bringing pramloads of them to all our social functions, and held a baby party every Christmas in the hall which had to be seen to be believed by anyone who doubted their being natural mothers of remarkable competence.

"Rules?—well, unfortunately, life is impossible without some, as I am sure you have discovered if you've ever played football, netball or any other game. Otherwise I might be tempted to strike Linda for dancing on her desk as I entered. Boredom?—well, boredom is rather like being in the bath; not much other folks can do for you, so you have to make the effort to get out of it yourself. Take an interest in things, even if you don't particularly like them, just as I do when I have to teach RK to young Rubble here. Find plenty of hobbies, creative ones where there's a lot to do—like Mr Figgin and his boats. Play as many different games before you're too old, like me."

"Was you ever young, sir?" Rubble inquired.

"No, Fred. I was born wrinkled and bald, just as you see me now; the only baby in Cudford Maternity Hospital wearing spectacles and smoking a pipe. The doctor handed me to my dear mother with the words, 'Congratulations, Mrs Mould; a bouncing baby boy of sixty-one. His false teeth are already visible and he gave vent to his birth scream in Latin. The nurse is warming a bottle of Scotch for his first feed. When you feel strong enough in a few days time he'll drive you home in the car before he goes off to work. I'll leave his pension book on your locker, so try to sit up while he makes the bed, then later on he can read to you'."

The class howled at Mr Mould's nonsense, but Mr Leonard was not amused. He whispered to Mr Mould, "Can you tell me how to control them when you're gone?"

"You must love them, Mr Leonard, not convert them. Give them ample work which is reasonably interesting—such as the history of their own area—but ensure it is within their capabilities. Given these basic requirements most of them will work like slaves for you—sorry, will work hard for themselves. They detest chaos, idleness and lack of authority, believe it or not. Throw in praise rather than censure, salt your lessons with humour, manifest your interest in every child even Fred. Most classroom problems we create ourselves, young man—too often we blame the pupils for our own shortcomings. You will quickly discover these unruly brats are for the most part delightful, easy-going, happy children who should give you much pleasure when you really get to know them."

"Thank you, Mr Mould. Anything else?—I'm desperate."

Mr Mould looked the teacher in the eye. "There is one more important item, sir, but being of a personal nature I do not relish giving it tongue—though in the past I have been obliged to advise student teachers of it when they have sought my counsel concerning their inability to control eleven-year-old children—but I do assure you only as a last resort."

Mr Leonard looked extremely worried. "You mean I've got B.O?"

"No, sir. I mean you've got W.C."

"That sounds even worse!"

"Just as one may presuppose that you would hesitate to attend a wedding in a diving-suit, so one may deduce that we attend school in teaching dress. Students from our Colleges of Education have arrived here on Teaching Practice in every garb, from formal to dustmen, from film star to struggling artist, from fashion model to hippy. I have discovered fat little men going into the ladies' toilet, and thin blondes going into the gents. A few have appeared in front of classes with tide marks visible on necks and arms, and one gentleman endeavoured to teach with both big toes exposed to the vulgar gaze.

"But you're behind the times, Mr Mould. Cap and gown went out years ago. Today people wear what they like."

"Precisely, sir. I am indeed behind the times. Unfortunately for us all, the pupils here are also behind the times. Sweet, old-fashioned kids that they are, they expect teachers to dress as teachers, not as road-sweepers of days past. You see, sir, the axiom that if one dresses like a tramp people will treat one like a tramp is as true today as ever it was—particularly in this school. Imagine the fate of a ship's captain who ignored the power of gold braid on his crew. Hence it is my unpleasant task to point out your Wrong Clothing, or to be more precise, inappropriate dress for the job."

"But this seems all wrong, Mr Mould—archaic," Mr Leonard protested.

"Indeed it is all wrong, sir, but it has been my lifelong burden to bring to people's attention the difference between what actually pertains in education, and what some folks think should pertain in education. I merely pass on to you the revealing comments and the adverse reactions I perceive during my years under the relentless scrutiny of our pupils. Those who write me off as an old fool should research this matter themselves, and discover whom the pupils respect and whom the pupils despise. They may be in for a few old-fashioned shocks to their pride."

We were interrupted by the entrance of Dr Collins, who bore in one hand a chased set of brass-and-copper fire-irons which normally decorated the hearth in his study, but which he was now carrying about the school because Mr Figgin was working next to his study and he did not wish them to reappear later as the stern-rail of a boat. Only last week Dr Collins had accidentally noticed that the brass plate on his door which read *Headmaster* was still there but could no longer be polished. Closer inspection disclosed that the metal had changed from brass to gold-painted wood, and that the door-handle itself had turned into plastic. This incident reminded the Head that his tea no longer came in on its copper tray but on a plywood tray similar to those being made by Mr Tadd's Third Year class.

"Ah, gentlemen, what a well-behaved class to be sure," Dr Collins beamed. "Sorry to interrupt your conference but I am looking for Mr Tadd. Mr Figgin tells me that when I gave him my pewter inkstand to repair last year he handed the job over to Mr Tadd. Although Mr Figgin provided me with a temporary replacement in perspex, I still hanker for the old pewter."

I said nothing because, no matter how he hankered, the Head would never see the inkstand again. Even as he stood there, his inkstand was revolving below the water-line on the Norfolk

Broads in an unrecognizable shape. Only his umbrella-stand was less retrievable, lying as it did on the bed of the Bass Strait, twenty miles off Tasmania, as one more lost anchor.

"Dear me, gentlemen, what an affluent society we live in," Dr Collins observed, looking through the classroom window to the boats lined up on trailers behind the staff's cars. "More and more of us seem to be taking up sailing these days, and I hear that Mr Figgin's boat club is booming. I count eight craft there in the car park alone."

How can you tell a man that he is looking at his training-ship?

"I have it on good authority that more of our lads gain apprenticeships to Cudford Shipyard than from any other school."

"The rest join either the Royal Navy or the Merchant Navy," I reminded him, "except Bob Fletcher who took up ship-breaking."

Dr Collins laughed absent-mindedly, like a man who has lost his drink in an empty pub. "All in order I trust, gentlemen," he inquired with roving eyes. "Nothing missing? Full complement of desks? Steel-window frames intact?"

We gave him the contented staff smile. "I just popped in to borrow a stick of chalk from Mr Leonard, sir, that's all. Then we began to chat about the pupils and how lucky we are to serve in a school like ours when one hears such awful tales about other schools up and down the country."

"Ah, Mr Mould, who knows better than you that my leadership here is not the whole story by any means—the rest of my loyal staff play their part too, you know. Oh well, I must be off in search of the elusive Mr Tadd."

When the door had closed, Mr Mould lit his pipe thoughtfully. "We could do worse than the old man, Peter. I pay him the highest compliment one can pay to any Head in the land—he means well, and doesn't poke his nose into the teaching side overmuch. My own nose doth scent the fragrance of coffee in the air, so let us to the staff room swift repair."

ELEVEN

Our annual Farewell Ball was always a glamorous occasion, except perhaps for the music, supplied alternately by pop records and the school band. The latter stuck to the slow definite rhythm of the waltz, led by petite Miss Orford on piano who employed head and arm to coordinate a motley collection of drums, brass and woodwind played by the boys and girls. The musicians stared hypnotically at their sheet music, performing with the robot deliberateness of those statue figures on the old Steam organs, occasionally blowing a wrong note through finger collision but making an excellent noise on the whole.

Standing over Miss Orford to turn the pages was giant Larry Hobbs, the boy whose long crush on the mistress was even more evident tonight because he had never seen so much of her in a strapless evening gown. Larry could not read music, simply turning the score when Miss Orford cued "Over!"—a request usually followed by "That's *The Mikado,* twit; turn back three."

Big Larry was the bane of Miss Orford's life, a self-appointed Protector who towered over her after school to growl his deep offer "Can I carry yer fings, miss?" in a bass voice we had all come to dread in the classroom, where the faulty acoustics boomed it into a foghorn off Sheerness. In order not to disturb adjacent classes Miss Orford begged him to whisper, but Larry's whisper seemed to come from so far down in his boots that I was reminded of the great gong of Peking.

At the moment Larry was dancing with his goddess, an awkward shambling giant unwittingly knocking hell out of her. Mr Mould was partnering the Head girl, a pretty maiden with a good brain who was not getting much attention from her teacher right now because he was bawling over to Crowhurst an unacademic order to turn down an unspecified bloody thing. Crowhurst, dancing with Mrs Collins and immaculate in his father's suit which displayed a great deal of wrist and ankle, failed to grasp what this terrible object was that had to be turned down until Mr Mould blocked his ears and pointed to the record-player.

Crowhurst was OC record-player for the evening, and, like his peers, considered anything below full blast as off. Nevertheless, in deference to Mr Mould's advanced age and partiality for kicking record-players out of rooms, he modified the volume to a tolerable level, then returned to the bliss of Mrs Collins' plump arms.

Was it possible, I asked myself, that these beautiful girls in their backless gowns, their youthful shoulders covered only by cascades of shimmering hair, were the same timid little toddlers who had crept into my classroom, all eyes and freckles, only five short years before? Was it possible that these slender beauties, half of them engaged, all with boyfriends, had prepared the sumptuous buffet awaiting us on long tables?

I found myself sitting next to Gloria, who had brought me a minute glass of shandy from the refreshment bar. "I wish you would stop putting your knee on my hand, Gloria," I chaffed her.

Gloria was the only girl wearing a short cocktail dress, on the grounds that her legs were like the National Gallery, for all the world to see. The world could also see a great deal more of Gloria because, apart from a heart locket hanging from a gold neck-band, she was not wearing much upstairs either.

"Please come and dance with me, sir?" she smiled, rising on the impossible stilts she wore in place of shoes. This record is a smoochie one and I've officially left school now."

Ignoring the possibility of my having to leave school, too, I held her as far away as possible and struck up a formal conversation as we swayed on the floor in the pendulum motion required today. Over Gloria's powerful hair-spray I read the posters of modern education adorning the walls: 'Your Baby in Two Parts; Part Three in Preparation.' 'How to Avoid an

Unwanted Baby,' under which somebody had inked 'Drive round it.'

"Are you feeling better tonight, Gloria?" I inquired. She had been absent for three days on the strength of her mum's note which read: 'Gloria has been away from school as I had a bad cold.' Gloria's notes always intrigued me over the years: 'Gloria couldn't come to school as she needed new shoes.' 'Gloria was off school as our dog got run over.' 'Can you give Gloria her mark and get the bread?' 'Gloria was away last week as we overslept.' 'Gloria is late for school as her Nan died unexpectedly.' 'I kept Gloria in bed yesterday after she come back from the butchers.' 'Gloria came home last night with a nasty head.' 'Gloria is in bed with another throat.' 'Gloria won't be back until that hand stops paying her off.' 'Gloria's ear has come back again only bigger.' 'The nurse says Gloria has a boil on her record card.' 'I am writing to let you know Gloria is in bed with the doctor.' 'Gloria came out in spots after I spoke to her.' 'She's got that rash on the brain.' 'Gloria broke her arm on the radio.' 'Gloria won't go out till her leg has gone.' 'I am worried about Gloria's nasty tongue.' 'Gloria has not been the same since she lost her tonsils in Birmingham.' But the note I shall always cherish read: 'Gloria's appetite is slowly coming back, so tonight I have give her a hot male in bed.'

"Oh, I feel really lovely, sir. I've grown into a woman at last."

We all experienced some trying times during her biological metamorphosis, such as eating in class to prevent her dying at her desk before dinner. I did not mind the kids eating in class provided they gave me one too, but I was unable to identify the noise issuing from below Gloria's desk. It was not the customary sweet wrapper or even a crisps bag, and to judge from Gloria's cheeks she might have been eating a toffee apple whole. Gliding silently to the rear of the classroom I was able to watch her unnoticed as she devoured a bread-and-butter pudding lying in oven foil on her lap.

I observed how some of Gloria's loveliness was rubbing off on my white shirt where she collapsed on me for the dance, and I experienced a definite sensation of dribbling in the chest region.

"I'm sorry I got to go now I got to go," she said. "I learnt a lot during the Fifth Year and I'm going to name my first baby after you, sir."

"Pook for a boy, Pooka for a girl?"

"No, sir, Peter or Petrol."

"So her full name will be Petroleum? I think its usually Petra, dear—short for Petrified."

"You always make me giggle, sir!"

'That's why I use so many shirts, dear."

"Oh, there's Mike arrived at last, sir—in't he lovely? I want you to meet him right away 'cos I've told him all about you."

I shook hands with a tall young man wearing a sailor suit and cap perched dead centre on his head. He walked and turned very stiffly, as though life was meant for keeping caps balanced on heads. He did not smile nor speak beyond "Orroight" in reply to my query about life in the navy. He looked a very tall twelve to me—which is a sign of old age in me, they say—and I discovered that when he was not concentrating on his cap at one end he was engrossed in a large consignment of boots at his other end. His only other diversion was a remarkably short cigarette butt halfway up which he contrived to hold and smoke to infinity by the very tips of his fingernails, so that an ash-tray would have been superfluous.

"Mike's in the navy, sir," Gloria informed me and Mike when I had run out of conversation. This invariably happened when old pupils returned to the school, as they so often did, dressed as firemen, nurses, soldiers or unemployed. After preliminary greetings of "Hallo, sir," and "Orroight", they dried up completely, staring at me while I racked my brain for small-talk remotely connected with their sojourn with us. Sometimes as many as five old boys would stare at me simultaneously while I struggled to recollect their names and forms before they returned in various disguises and with shorn locks. It was always a delight to discover that the big smart police cadet in front of me had once been thin little Gary Lester of the long hair and dirty jeans, or that the near-bald Corporal whose cap peak covered his eyes and half the nose as he stood rigidly to attention for an informal chat in my classroom was none other than young Colin Swaine, late yob of the Fourth Year, now unsmiling robot in tanks.

They made me feel like Mr Chips the day he shuffled into retirement, but it was rewarding to see in what affection they held the old place and appreciated what we had tried to do for them.

Leaving Gloria with her beloved, I bumped into Crowhurst.

"I want to ask you a special favour, sir," he beamed archly.

"You can't dance with me, Crowhurst; I'm booked."

"No, sir, it's for my dad."

"I'm not dancing with him either."

"You see, sir, my dad says you're the best teacher in the school."

"You are merely repeating what I have so often told you. And in any case, how can he know when I'm the only member of staff who teaches him?"

Crowhurst laughed knowingly, head on one side and teeth to the fore. "Well, sir, he says could you go on marking the work he does, even though I've left?"

"But there won't be any more work to mark."

"Dad says could you keep setting it just the same, sir?"

"But you'll be gone, laddie."

"Ah, but my little brother comes next term, sir. Then there'll be five more for you eventually, sir."

Crowhurst broke this news as though his family's function in life was to keep me supplied with Crowhursts like a recruiting station.

"The way my mum's going, sir, you won't run out of Crowhursts until you retire. One more in the oven right now, sir. Could be twins."

"But I suppose your dear old mum is getting on a bit these days, eh?"

"Oh yes, sir, she's not far off twenty-three now."

"Fancy you having a mother older than yourself, Crowhurst. I bet you wish she was still seven, like when you were born."

"Dad married again, sir. Third time actually. That's why I'm so brainy."

I made a mental note not to teach Mr Crowhurst anything except birth-control or sterilization. Some of the biggest breeders in Cudford came under our catchment area, sending wave upon wave of retarded offspring to us at yearly intervals, until Mr Mould was on his knees in the staff room imploring the Almighty to bless the human race with thirty years of impotence, so we could get our breath back. He cited the streets black with children every day at four o'clock, each one of whom would need a partner and a house in order to produce even more children. Yet as the new schools were built they proved too small to cope with the birth-rate. Our own school had been planned for six hundred but we housed a thousand, and were now expanding to accommodate thirteen hundred in an effort to contain the flood.

Since I had joined the school I witnessed the meadows and woods literally disappear and emerge as housing estates right round the horizon. Even our own playing-field was gradually vanishing under new teaching blocks and terrapins, as if man prefers to occupy every inch of the globe rather than control population growth. Yet the waiting list for houses is not shorter, but longer than it ever was. A dog never catches his own tail. Build more houses they cry, so they build more houses to breed more people who need more houses. Mr Mould impressed on our pupils the sensible slogan of Two Will Do, explaining that if we limited our families to two children per couple we could save the day and start to build a better world for everybody. Otherwise, just as our cities are already stinking and choked by traffic, so will our land become infested with ailing humans.

"Fortunately for me," Mr Mould was saying at the buffet table, "I have only about ten years left, when I shall retire gracefully to Cudford Cemetery where I can lie down and admire the beautiful flowers. Until the horde of humanity trample my grave in search of more land and I learn that I am to serve future generations as part of the footings for one more tower block full of breeding, fighting, robbing, murdering, discontented, corrupted, destroying, lying, lustful, greedy *Homo Sapiens. Homo Sapiens!*— what a supremely ironic joke to call us Wise Men, when it should be *Homo Nullorum Hominum,* Men unfitted for our planet."

"This is supposed to be a jolly occasion, Mr Mould, for those about to leave school," I reminded him.

Mr Mould swigged the shandy and puffed his pipe vigorously. "A timely reminder, Pook, for which much thanks. It would be an even jollier occasion if some of the staff were leaving too. For it is our lot to witness modern education dividing teachers into separate camps of Administrators and Non-administrators, whereby we perceive the Headmaster and his immediate subordinates remote from the classroom, cut off from the children—yet imposing upon us those academic theories they garner from every fashionable crackpot under whose spell they stumble."

"But someone has to do the admin. chores, Mr Mould."

Mr Mould gave me a look bordering on sympathy. "Would not your simple layman suppose that the best teachers were the most highly paid, therefore most competent to instruct our children? Would not your simple layman be surprised to find that this is precisely what they do not do? Would not your simple layman be astonished to discover that your supposedly best staff, earning in excess of £4000 per annum are engaged in such tasks as compiling duty rota lists, organizing the staff car park, and similar mundane chores which could be performed by a probationary teacher or a clerk?"

"What we need right now is a simple layman, I guess."

"Ah Pook, there was a time not so long ago when every senior member of staff—Headmaster included—felt duty-bound to spend some portion of his day inside the classroom, for obvious reasons. But your new breed, Pook, consider the office and the study more important. They seem bent on pulling as many staff from the classroom as possible, in order to surround themselves with a protective wall of administrators. Outworks to keep the children at bay, if you like, as Dr Collins does."

"Did I hear my name mentioned?" Dr Collins called across the sausage-rolls where he was trying to keep Crowhurst at bay.

"You did indeed, sir," Mr Mould boomed, angered by his own rhetoric. "I was saying what a pity it is that top staff like yourself no longer keep in touch with the pupils by actually taking their lessons in the classroom, as was formerly standard practice. I was explaining how such omission is detrimental to teacher and child alike in the development of education throughout the nation. I was bemoaning the fact that senior staff are now relegated to the role of clerks, whereby it may cost the country £4000 per annum to check stationery invoices."

"Please sir, I always thought Headmasters weren't allowed to teach," Crowhurst cried, under the impression he was defending Dr Collins.

"Silence, Crowhurst—go and attend to the record-player," Dr Collins barked, suddenly smiling after he had spoken, to show Crowhurst he was not cross.

"Out of the mouths of babes and sucklings, sir," Mr Mould snapped.

"Now hold hard, Mr Mould; nobody knows better than you the multiplicity of my functions in the modern educational milieu. For example, someone has to deal with the mass of paperwork now essential to the performance of the simplest undertaking."

"I take your point, sir, because we have the same business at home where my wife does it. She calls it housekeeping, sir."

"So, as I am required at all hours of the day, how can I possibly engage to teach in the classroom?"

"I recall a parallel situation during the war, sir, when my prime objective was to get out of the front line in order to defeat Hitler from Whitehall. . . ."

Unobtrusively I stole away, that the two veterans might continue their weekly row in peace. As I passed Mr Figgin, resplendent in his new uniform of Commodore to Cudford School Yacht Club, a hand slipped into mine so gently that for a moment I thought Gloria had deserted Mike. But they were holding each other up on the dance floor, oblivious to matters academic. I discovered the arm led to Karen, a beautiful Karen I had not seen before—hair loose about bare shoulders, eyes sparkling to outstrip the jewels at her throat. It struck me as strange why women only bring out their other self at parties and weddings, instead of delighting us with their femininity all the time. I kissed her because it seemed the natural thing to do.

"Sorry I'm late, Peter," she whispered. "The blessed zip broke."

"So I see, dear. Still, stick this rose in the centre and don't breathe too deeply."

"The zip's at the back, idiot!"

I said nothing because women are funny about these things, like when I was a student earning holiday money on Cudford beach. My last job of the day was to carry the little bathing tent up the ramp to the store, but one evening when I did this I looked round and was appalled to see Hilda Longbothem standing there naked, screaming at me for the tent back.

As I took Karen in my arms for the dance Mr Whittle staggered by, having his promotion waltz with the Head's wife, handicapped by his misinterpretation of the waltz as containing four beats instead of three and finding it difficult to dispose of the surplus steps he built up. Mrs Collins smiled serenely throughout, despite being surrounded by so much feet, standing almost still while Whittle encircled her like several Indians dancing round a totem pole. In passing I gave her my special smirk of sympathy reserved for ladies compelled to take part in Big Chief Whittle's war dance.

Over in the far corner I observed Commodore Figgin and Captain Tadd examining the school trophy cabinet with unnatural interest, especially the former, who, despite the glass doors, preferred to look at the exhibits through the keyhole. Captain Tadd admired the cups by rubbing his hand up and down the mahogany sides of the cabinet, then actually smelling the wood like a short-sighted lumberjack. When I lost them from view the two men were testing the whole structure for weight, and it occurred to me that next term we might well end up with twenty-eight wooden cups displayed on a wall shelf.

"You haven't said yet how I look, Peter," Karen fished.

"Gorgeous, dear. I think all of you looks beautiful."

"What do you mean, all of me?"

"Well, you know how it is, darling . . . there's a lot of you on view tonight to praise."

"Such as?"

"Well, your lovely gold slippers. You're the nicest thing since tubeless tyres."

"Och, mon, how you turn a lassie's head wi' your soft tongue. Gie us a wee kiss on ma flat-iron, ye big daft pilloch."

Directly I heard Karen lapse into porridge patter I knew she was mine, and I marvelled at this magnetic influence I had over women once they had got used to my pan. With the quick familiarity of her sex Karen was already re-erecting my nose where it used to be, and arranging my lips so they were one above the other all the way along. Finally, with her free hand, she carefully adjusted my left eyelid until it was open just like the one on the other side.

"Who's a pretty boy now?" I croaked in a parrot voice.

"Shut up and don't use your lips, Peter. I want to kiss you properly. Don't move your face and spoil it."

"Would it help if I switched the lights off?"

"Stop worrying about your looks, darling—you know I can't stand pretty men."

"No wonder you're crazy about me then."

"I love you because you are different, Peter."

"Nobody else had to stop the Welsh fifteen with his face."

"Well, say what you like, I wouldn't have you any other way."

"You have to say that because you're not a plastic surgeon."

"On top of which you are the most unromantic cuss I've ever met."

"No good playing the great lover when girls ask you if you've been run over lately. Hilda Longbothem reckons if I witnessed a car smash they'd put me in the ambulance first."

Karen sighed deeply. "Oh, Peter, what a terrible thing you have about your looks."

"Yes, dear, it's my face. . . ."

"Shut up! I'm going to show you how it's you who counts, not your face."

"You're going to invite me to a masked ball?"

"And I'm determined to get rid of this horrid chip on your shoulder."

"I'll look worse with no head."

"Because what you desperately need right now is a woman's

tender love to restore your confidence in yourself."

"But where can we find such a woman, Karen?"

"Well, you certainly won't find her by peering over my shoulder towards Europe."

"You mean we could find one in Britain?"

"Provided I wear a flashing light like a buoy. You'll scarcely need binoculars tonight if you shade your eyes with your hand and scan the horizon just below your nose. But if you prefer the excitement of the chase I'll hide under your jacket."

"Karen, surely you don't mean you?"

"Well, I'm certainly not doing all this graft for some other woman. What else do you want—radar?"

"But I couldn't expect you to make such a sacrifice just for me, darling."

"Don't worry about the future—we need all our strength at the moment just to locate each other. If ever you write a romantic novel make sure the happy ending comes in the first chapter. They'll need the rest of the book to find out how they can fall in love with each other."

"But you're so beautiful, Karen; you mustn't throw away the best years of your life on me."

"The best years of my life were before I met you. Now I've got to pay for them. So pile your lips on top of each other horizontally so I can kiss you properly to seal the bargain, then try not to let them collapse at the far end. And if you act up again I'll hit you over the head with an Oscar."

How can you resist women when they coax you so sweetly with their feminine wiles and subtle flattery? I could not bear to think of Karen's unhappiness without me, deprived of her mission like a mountain guide sent to work in Holland.

"O.K., darling, you win," I sighed, "I'm all yours. The things we do for women—still, they're worth it really. None but the fair deserve the brave."

"A thousand thanks, master. What would my lord like first,

my father's camels or the seven sons?"

"Make it Scotch all round, honey."

Karen took me in her arms in front of the whole staff and kissed me on all the lips I could muster at such short notice.

Oddly enough, the embrace was instantly recorded by the flash of a Polaroid camera, followed soon afterwards by a familiar voice crying "40p each, 40p each! Your actual snog in colour, only 40p a time!"

Karen gazed fondly into my good eye. "Nothing you can do about him now he's left school, darling."

I smiled sportingly and kissed her cheek. "I know he's left school, sweetie, but he hasn't left the school premises yet. You may be the first girl to drink champagne out of a camera."

It's true about school days being the happiest days of your life—especially for the staff.

THE END

If you enjoyed reading
"The Teacher's Hand-Pook",
you can follow more of Pook's adventures in
"Pook's Viking Virgins".

An extract follows.

POOK'S VIKING VIRGINS

ONE

I noticed Angela the moment I checked her onto the blue and gold coach at Ostend—one of those leggy brunettes whom weaker men find so attractive that they suddenly become all eyeballs and good manners.

Fortunately for me I had little interest in girls, especially right now when I was bound for a cultural tour of Scandinavia to study male Vikings of the ninth century and no damned nonsense about Sexy Sweden, Naughty Norway and Daring Denmark, to quote from Standing Orders issued by my beloved Olga.

In fact Olga was smiling sweetly down upon me from the coach window even now, so I gave her my dedicated historian smirk to let her see I had barely observed Angela except as a fare-paying tick in column 5 of my passenger sheet.

At last Honners stopped screaming along the jetty in a shrill mixture of English and O-level French to the effect that if certain constipated snails didn't hurry to the coach they would have the pleasure of doing our Grand Tour on foot after retrieving their luggage from the sea.

"What did you think of Angela Bray, the fantastic sex job on high heels, Peter?" Honners inquired, leering at her legs as she was handed up the coach steps by Eddie, our driver, two Canadians and a New Zealander. I smiled sadly at my short friend.

"You'd think she had rickets, the way those impressionable fellows are helping her into the coach. Fortunately I am made of sterner stuff, my mind elevated solely upon Viking research for Olga. To me she's just a seat-filling statistic."

"So you've got no chance on this trip, what with Olga and your duties as our multi-lingual courier, as specified in the brochure."

"Come to mention the brochure, Honners, how is it that the pictures show our coach packed with gorgeous Angelas, yet we've only got one, not counting Olga, of course? The other passengers look pretty passé to me. In fact one old dear up front must have thought we were travelling by stagecoach. She's ticked her form in the column for ages running to three figures."

Honners stood to attention indignantly. "That grande dame happens to be my illustrious ancestor, the Lady Millicent Pilkington-Goldberg of treasured memory."

"Why, is she dead?"

"Very much alive, serf. Although now in her nineties my great-aunt has already booked next year for our Torrid Tour of Tantalizing Turkey, a formidable bottom-bashing ride into Aromatic Asia of Antiquity."

"So she gets a free holiday every year."

I threw in this barb because Honners himself was a director of Cudford Continental Coach Company, and had employed me on a cutprice salary because I was experiencing slight embarrassment as a celebrated novelist in that I was unable to eat regularly, plus the fact that the football pools had proved singularly unrewarding of late. My exciting second dividend win had occurred that week when there were nineteen score draws, reducing my prize-money fortune to a postal-order for seventy-five pence—a poor return for my £1 Bullseye Perm investment.

My salary had been eroded because Olga would not let me go to Scandinavia unchaperoned, with the result that Honners had kindly given her a Special Students Concessionary Voucher and deducted £200 from my wages. When I protested he explained how many men actually volunteered to do the job without pay because of the generous tips that went with it. One Ben Grossmith had even offered Honners a substantial fee to secure the post but fortunately for me Honners had put friendship above financial inducement.

"All aboard and off we go!" Honners shouted, quickly

checking heads. "Only one empty seat and we pick the guy up at Hamburg. Eyes down for a full house! Pull her out, Eddie, and pick up the Antwerp autobahn. Remember it cuts down heart-failure among the passengers if you drive on the right. Only another 3,000 miles to go and you'll all be safely home thinking about the most wonderful holiday of your lives, folks."

"This one should be pretty good too, Honners," I observed.

"Ah, Peter, let 'em have your running commentary right now before they nod off. Galvanize them into a frenzy of interest and clicking cameras."

I realized this was not going to be easy because many of the passengers had been travelling since dawn to arrive at Ostend for our 7 p.m. rendezvous in the big Commodore coach. It was now 8 p.m. and some of the holidaymakers were obviously suffering from that exhaustion which is never mentioned in the brochures. In Brochureland nobody is ever ill, let alone tired. Everybody is young, beautiful and exploding with energy, waving to the laughing gendarmes, rubbing one another with suntan lotion and dancing with the delighted street traders.

No pictures of weary travellers, heads back, eyes shut, mouths open, gently snoring in the sleep of exhaustion, some with heavy colds, some with Gyppo tummies or hopelessly costive, as the rain lashes down on the table umbrellas outside the hotel.

I produced the guide-book I had brought along for the purpose, unhooked the mike from over Eddie's head and began to read in a kind of euphoric voice I copied from television commercials.

"Welcome to another marvellous tour of foreign exploration with Cudford Continental Coach Company Tours, ladies and gentlemen," I began, glancing through the windows to the drab, flat landscape of Belgium, already growing dim in the August twilight.

"Can we have the heaters on, please," came a shout from

Miss Bliss in seat 21, more in the shape of an order than a request.

"How do you shut these blessed ventilation nozzles, courier?" A cry of despair from Mr Salt in seat 26. "I can already feel my neuralgia coming on."

Along both sides of the coach numerous hands were up, experimenting with the ventilation nozzles over every seat in efforts to close them. Mr Salt was stuffing his with tissue handkerchiefs against the draughts caused by Personalized Ventilation, as the brochure described the scientific breakthrough of sealing the windows and giving everybody their own fresh air through an adjustable tube.

"The major feature of every coach tour is trying to close these damned vents," Honners swore as he struggled with all he could reach. "You're driving past the great battlefields of history and all they're worried about are these blasted little plastic blowers that give them neuralgia in the evenings and heat bumps during the day. They'll be twisting and pulling and bashing them right through Europe, not to mention stuffing paper up them—that's why most of the things are broken already."

"I'll just fix Angela's for her, Honners."

'No you don't! I'll work right round the coach while you take their minds off draughts with the travel talk. Then wait for tomorrow when some want the roof windows opened and some don't. That'll really drive you potty."

I opened my book once more to flood the coach with learning for the benefit of those passengers still awake. "We are now passing through the prosperous little country of Belgium, ladies and gentlemen, with a population of eight million souls ruled over by King Leopold the Third, who ascended the throne in 1934. . . ."

Honners suddenly stopped fighting the air-vents and snatched the book from me. "Published in 1936!" he gasped. "We're not cracking along at a hundred kilometres per hour to be in time for the Battle of Waterloo, you know."

"Poor Peter," Olga volunteered. "He can't afford anything new. He's still using the first edition of the *Writers' and Artists' Yearbook.* As for his dictionary, he thinks music has a K on the end."

"Here take mine," Honners snapped. "It's the 1977 guide, so I hope you can read this modern print."

We arrived at the Harbour Hotel, Antwerp, dead on 10 p.m., where Eddie and I had to fish out forty-five suitcases from the boot of the coach, an operation which turned the hotel lobby into a sea of leather. Having successfully throttled all movement in or out of the hotel, I received the room numbers from Reception and chalked each case with its final destination upstairs.

This chore so bushed me that I lay on my bed like an injured weightlifter after the Olympics until Eddie told me that dinner would be served at 11 p.m. sharp—that is to say, ten minutes ago. Consequently I was the last to arrive at table, and as Olga was surrounded by the Canadian party I had no option but to sit next to Angela. Nevertheless, I bore up bravely, and tired as I was I consumed all I could get of the appetizing food served by this magnificent hotel. Thick soup, with seconds, a huge chicken salad, and mixed fruits.

Angela felt thirsty when the wine waiter arrived so I ordered two tonic waters and threw a hundred franc note on the tray— every penny I possessed in Belgian currency—and received forty francs change. In order to take her mind off strong drink I asked her to dance, for I had noticed that Olga was already on the floor with an outsize American.

"All part of the Cudford Continental Coach Company's entertainments service," I laughed gaily to let her see I was versatile and still capable of standing up after the longest day of my life.

"You're certainly a marvellous dancer, Peter," she smiled.

I shrugged modestly. "Nothing really, dear—just natural talent plus years of practice. But a man is no good without the right partner—you move like a dream. We'll dance our way right round Scandinavia."

"You are lucky to be a travel courier, Peter. I suppose you've done this trip dozens of times, yet you don't seem a bit bored."

"There are two good reasons why I'm not bored, honey, and the big one is you."

"Oh! I like that. What's the other?"

"I've never been to Scandinavia before. In fact I've never been a courier before, and right now I'm suffering from suitcase stricture of the back muscles. That's why I have to hold you so tightly or I might collapse."

Just then Olga passed us quite close, smiling delightedly to see me doing my duty as courier so I smiled back to let her know I was nothing if not a worker. I thought how lucky I was to be so strong with women, dancing with Angela as coolly as I carried the suitcases. I thoroughly agreed with the feminist movement fighting for women's rights and making themselves unattractive to men, who, unlike me, were ever ready to fall for a pretty face and make fools of themselves. In fact I had thought of joining the movement myself if the ladies would accept members of the weaker sex. One thing was certain, Angela was so pretty that she provided a real challenge to my icy indifference to the wiles of women.

Angela nestled in my arms as though she did not sense what kind of a tough male she had encountered. "May I ask you rather an intimate question, Peter?" she whispered in my ear.

"You can ask me anything, honey—I go with the tariff," I purred. Here was a girl who didn't believe in wasting time.

"I do hope you won't think it's too personal of me when we've only just met." . . .

. . . Continued in "Pook's Viking Virgins", which can be ordered from all good bookshops or direct from Emissary Publishing